Books by Robert Nathan

NOVELS
> *Sir Henry* (1955)
> *The Train in the Meadow* (1953)
> *The Innocent Eve* (1951)
> *The Married Look* (1950)
> *The River Journey* (1949)
> *Long after Summer* (1948)
> *Mr. Whittle and the Morning Star* (1947)
> *But Gently Day* (1943)
> *The Sea-Gull Cry* (1942)
> *They Went On Together* (1941)
> *Tapiola's Brave Regiment* (1941)
> *Portrait of Jennie* (1940)
> *Winter in April* (1938)
> *Journey of Tapiola* (1938)
> *The Enchanted Voyage* (1936)
> *Road of Ages* (1935)
> *One More Spring* (1933)
> *Jonah* (1925)

AN OMNIBUS
> *The Barly Fields* (1938)–CONTAINING
>> *The Fiddler in Barly*
>> *The Woodcutter's House*
>> *The Bishop's Wife*
>> *The Orchid*
>> *There Is Another Heaven*

POEMS
> *The Green Leaf* (1950)
> *The Darkening Meadows* (1945)
> *Morning in Iowa* (1944)
> *Dunkirk* (1941)
> *A Winter Tide* (1940)
> *Selected Poems* (1935)

THEATER
> *Jezebel's Husband and The Sleeping Beauty* (1953)

NON-FICTION
> *Journal for Josephine* (1943)

These are BORZOI BOOKS, *published by* ALFRED A. KNOPF

SIR HENRY

SIR HENRY

BY

ROBERT NATHAN

NEW YORK
ALFRED A. KNOPF
1955

L. C. catalog card number: 54–12039

THIS IS A BORZOI BOOK,
PUBLISHED BY ALFRED A. KNOPF, INC.

FIRST EDITION

CONTENTS

Chap. 1 *in which we meet an ordinary, working knight, his reluctant hound, and his horse* 3

Chap. 2 *in which we are surprised by a dragon* 13

Chap. 3 *. . . and by the dragon's ward* 22

Chap. 4 *in which plans are made, heroism is discussed, and a rabbit is outraged* 28

Chap. 5 *in which Sir Henry and the Lady Alisane stop for tea with a sorcerer* 39

Chap. 6 *in which Sir Henry adds somewhat embarrassingly to his entourage* 49

Chap. 7 *wherein we are introduced to several different points of view* 61

Chap. 8 *in which our travelers reach the city of Chichester* 69

Chap. 9 *. . . and rest there in good comfort* 78

[v]

CONTENTS

Chap. 10   *wherein Sir Henry meets a dispirited knight, and Meghan meets with a disappointment*   88

Chap. 11   *concerning the great battle in the forest*   98

Chap. 12   *concerning natural man; and of Sir Henry's arrival at Devizes*   110

Chap. 13   *of the Tournament of Beauty; and some lectures upon an interesting subject*   124

Chap. 14   *in which Manfred experiences a grief*   137

Chap. 15   *in which Sir Henry is met with silence*   146

Chap. 16   *wherein Sir Henry builds his house*   157

Chap. 17   *concerning Sir Henry's last quest*   167

Chap. 18   *wherein he meets Himself*   181

SIR HENRY

CHAPTER

i

in which we meet an ordinary, working knight,

his reluctant hound, and his horse

Sir HENRY rested his horse, Ponderer, by Indal Water, where it rounded in clear green pools among the boulders beneath Hart's Hill. He rested himself, also, on the moss along the river bank, grateful for the water-coolness and for the leaf shade of the woods. His dog, Manfred, lay beside him, and his spear, sword, and helmet reclined at his side.

Sir Henry was not a young man; and his hound, Manfred, was not young, either. The knight's armor was conventional, rather heavy, and slightly old-fashioned; his sword, which had started out as a brave two-hander, had, from much use and honing, lost half its heft; his horse was solid, and needed grooming. On his shield was executed, in tempera, a sun semi-risant, gules; and the single device: *Esperans*. The point of his spear needed sharpening.

In short, one would have said that here was a solid, down-to-earth, workaday knight, engaged in making his living.

But despite the length of his service as a knight-errant, Sir Henry had accumulated very little of the world's treasure. In character, he was inclined to be cautious, and given to a slight melancholy; his main fault lay in thinking that happiness lay always somewhere else, instead of where he happened to be.

Manfred, the hound, gazed patiently up at his master; then, putting his head down, lapped a little water from the stream. It was not very filling but it was something. A trout, hiding under a stone, watched the dog's tongue as it broke through the arch of water-and-air above him. It seemed like a great mystery, and filled the little fish with religious fears. "After all," he said to a friend who was passing by, "we know very little of what lies beyond; and we should worship what we do not know." "Nonsense," said his friend, "there is nothing beyond, except an absence of water.

"Do you want to worship an absence?"

The first fish did not reply. But it seemed to him that there was, at least, neither cruelty nor injustice in an absence; and that an actual Presence in the world above was just as mysterious as nothing at all.

With a sigh Sir Henry reached up and took down the leather pouch which hung from his saddle. He knew only too well what he would find in it: a little cheese, and some hard bread; a few silver coins; and a woolen stomacher for the ache. He had little else in the way of possessions; a silver cup, an iron pot, a small knife or dagger; a cloak, a doublet, a blanket, and some woolen underwear.

It was enough for an ordinary working knight; it was all he needed, actually; but he did wish he had a little fat meat, or an egg; something besides cheese.

Still, he was grateful for the shade, and for Indal Water; and he was satisfied to be a knight, to be free, and to have adventures.

As a matter of fact, there was no help for it; he had been born into knighthood, and could not possibly have been anything else. A hero's life was all there was for Sir Henry, with its aches and pains, and with the small cheese, the hard bread, and a sup of Indal Water.

"Of course," he remarked reflectively, to no one in particular, "if there were some conceivable end to it—like a decent castle of my own, and a rich wife, agreeably endowed; but I am sure there is nothing like that for me in the foreseeable future. One must have luck, for that sort of thing."

He leaned back and clasped his hands behind his head. The leaves cast a dapple of shadow on his face; he felt cool and lazy, and he reflected on his life, which nevertheless seemed to him, on the whole, reasonably satisfactory. "It would be more so," he thought, "except for the fighting."

Not that he was a coward; when it was time to fight, he fought. But, unlike some of his colleagues, he didn't enjoy it, and often suffered from nose-bleed and a headache afterwards. In addition, the sight of blood distressed him; most of all, his own.

However, there was only one way to win esteem in the world in which he lived, and that was to fight for it. "The world's heroes have always been men of force and might," he concluded.

It was peaceful by Indal Water, and Sir Henry began to feel drowsy. "But," he thought, "in the long winter evenings, when the green spring and the hot summer of life are past, one needs a companion with whom to relive, in memory, the good years." And in his dreamy mind he saw himself before his own fire, in his own castle, going over again, with his wife, the triumphant battles of the past. "There was Sir Pelham," he imagined himself saying; "with whom I battled for several hours, and had a headache all next day. And there was Sir Agravaine; we fought the Cloying Beast together. And there was the Lady Malinda. . . ."

Sir Henry sighed. "One has luck," he remarked, "or one has not."

At his feet, Manfred also drowsed. Birds sang in the forest, the river made small water sounds, the air smelled of earth and moss. The tiny, innumerable creatures of earth went about their important lives; ants rushed out from their cities and back again, bees flew like arrows into the blossoms, and mice looked out from under leaves, with wary, jewel-like eyes. A frog snapped his rubber tongue at a fly; and in the pool by the stone, the trout said to his friend:

"There are creatures beyond us; for I have seen their shadows. They move as we move, but not in water. Not being in water, they cannot breathe."

"Do they lay eggs?" asked his friend. The trout shook his head. "They are altogether spiritual," he said.

"Manfred," said a voice. The mastiff opened one eye and looked around. It was a soprano voice, and not familiar. "What is it?" he asked.

The bird sat on the branch a little to one side, but not very high. It was quite an ordinary bird, a female crested flycatcher. "Manfred," she said.

"Yes?" he replied. She was too far away to eat, and he had never thought that conversations with birds were particularly rewarding. At the same time, they did have a way of coming up with interesting bits of information from time to time. "What is it now?" he asked wearily.

"There's a dragon," she said. "Be careful."

Manfred gave a yawn. "There are always dragons," he remarked. "Is this the lonesome kind? or is he attached to something?"

"A maiden," said the bird.

Manfred sighed. "I'm not surprised," he said. "It's time we met something of the sort. I suppose Sir Henry will be pleased."

"Just the same," said the bird, "I'd tell him to be careful."

"What's the good of that?" said Manfred. "He won't listen to me. I have no influence."

"Well," said the bird doubtfully—"a big dog like you?"

The hound replied, not without a certain melancholy dignity:

"Dogs do what men tell them to do. Men never do what dogs tell them to do. This is one of the First Laws. . . . With cats, it's altogether different. Cats never do what people tell them to. No cat ever does what he's told. On the contrary—to get along with cats, people have to behave the way their cats want them to. That's why people think that cats are smart—instead of realizing that they are, on the contrary, stubborn, stupid, selfish, egotistical, greedy, lazy, and unbearable. Besides, they have no language; and have obstinately refused to learn English. Be glad you're a bird."

"Not while there are cats around," said the fly-catcher. "Be glad you're a dog."

"Oh well," said Manfred; "I can't help it, in any case. But don't think it's fun to be a knight's hound. Do you know what I've had to eat, in the last forty-eight hours?"

The bird shook her head. "There are a lot of delightful flies about," she declared; "and then, there's poppy seed. . . ." She gave a small, delicious sigh. "But perhaps you don't care for either?" she added anxiously.

"I have had," declared Manfred heavily, "two bites of cheese."

"I can see," said the bird sympathetically, "where two bites of cheese might not go very far. . . . However, cheer up. There's a dragon ahead, with a maiden. You may end up as part of a meal, of course—a dragon's meal; and then your troubles will be over. A dragon's digestive juices are very strong. But if—and . . . mind you, I say if—your master were to overcome the beast—why then you'll have a mistress—and you're bound to fare better."

"I am?" asked Manfred.

"Certainly. Do you think a maiden or a damsel would be satisfied with a little cheese, and some branch water? No, my friend; you'll see some changes made. Once a woman is in the picture . . . look for something fancy."

Manfred licked his lips; he could feel the saliva rising in his mouth. "You mean—steaks?" he croaked. "And stews? And short ribs?"

The bird looked down at him in surprise.

"Who said anything about short ribs?" she asked. And she added comfortably:

"Salads, my friend; salads. With whipped cream, and candied cherries. And poppy seeds."

ii

in which we are surprised by a dragon

THE flycatcher was quite right; there was a dragon. He—or she (there is always that question with dragons)—had its den, or lair, about a mile downstream, in a darksome thicket of trees, very leafy and shadowy, and near a deep pool, good for fishing, and swimming. But it was, to all practical purposes, a private pool; for no one—and nothing—cared to go swimming with a dragon.

It was waiting in front of its cave, sniffing the air, and smoking slightly at the nostrils. Roughly thirty-point-eight in length, of which four sevenths were tail, scaly, horned, with red eyes and a forked tongue, with strong hooked claws, but without wings, this mythical but present monster (one of the reptile family) waited for its dinner, which approached on horseback through the forest glades, humming a tune as it came.

The maiden also waited and dreamed. She dreamed of the knight who was to rescue her; and amused herself meanwhile by stringing together a necklace of old bits of armor, which she had found from time to time in the woods near the cave. Sir Henry was not the first knight who had come riding by; and looking at him, she hoped he would not be the last, but she was resigned to whatever happened. Her life with the dragon was not disagreeable; she had a small room of her own, with a bed, and a shelf for her collection; she had a silk scarf, and combs for her hair; but although she was not uncomfortable, she felt that she was not fulfilling her destiny.

It is only fair to say that Sir Henry was taken by

surprise. Riding quietly through the forest, in the late afternoon light, savoring the sweet smell of leaf-mold under foot, the warm fragrance of the day's good sun upon the leaves, a dragon was furthest from his thoughts. And Manfred's warning had gone—as Manfred had known it would—unheeded; the dog's short, sharp barks merely mystified his master, who suggested that he make less noise.

"Ah," said the dragon, "hm." It was a sort of rumble; but it stopped Sir Henry short. Ponderer also stopped, as did Manfred. Sir Henry and Manfred sat, and the horse stood; and all three looked at the dragon, which gazed back at them with an enigmatic expression.

The maiden, or damsel, also peered out at them, from an opening in her room, which served as a casement. Her name was Alisane, and she was of French extraction, though distantly. She had always expected to be rescued and married—or at least engaged—to a very parfit gentle knight; Sir Henry struck her as a compromise. Her glance fell upon Manfred, and she withdrew with a shudder; "What a starveling!" she thought; "his master does not feed him. I doubt if he would keep me in knightly style, though he has a kind face, or at least not an unkind one, and patient, but slightly mournful."

Manfred also had taken a good look at Alisane during the moment she had shown herself at the casement; and he felt depressed. "She does not look like a very hearty eater," he thought. And gazing mournfully at his master, he gave a low whine. "Must we go on with this?" he tried to say. But Sir Henry misread him completely.

"What?" he cried; "are you afraid of dragons?

"Come, sir! Up and at him!"

And he gave an encouraging shout. At the same time, he tried to remember what the best authorities had to say about dragon-fighting. It was some time since he had actually fought a dragon, and it had been considerably smaller than this one. And when he had fought the Cloying Beast, Sir Agravaine had been with him.

"Faint heart ne'er won fair lady," he observed.

The dragon gave a snort. "Have you seen her?" he asked—if it was a he.

Sir Henry was startled. Actually, he had not even known that a damsel was involved, and was merely making a remark, thinking that it was expected of him, and to keep his courage up. "I don't believe it matters," he said stiffly, and he added, a little doubtfully:

"This sort of thing is expected of me."

"Well," said the dragon, "why? After all, even if it comes off well for you—which is unlikely—it won't be pleasant. The very least you can expect is a nosebleed; and you know how that is. So why not simply forget the whole thing, and go quietly about your business, somewhere else?"

"Because you are there," said Sir Henry, "like a mountain, or some other natural fact; and being there, have to be climbed."

"I am not a mountain," said the dragon; "and I would not advise you to try to climb me."

And he added in brisk tones:

"Might I have the names of your next of kin?"

Sir Henry grew pale, but replied in as firm a voice as possible: "I am Henry of Brentwood, knight. My father was Sir Tiffany of The Glen, and my mother was an enchantress."

"Nonsense," said the dragon. "Your mother was a kitchen wench for King Uther Pendragon. I know all about her."

"She enchanted my father," said Sir Henry simply, "and the enchantment was strong enough to bring me into the world."

So saying, he kicked his horse, meaning to advance on the dragon at a smart trot. Instead, the horse backed away a little.

"Forward," said Sir Henry.

And he brought the flat of his sword down on Ponderer's rump. The startled animal gave a jump, and the sword flew out of Sir Henry's hand, and landed on the ground.

"Damn," said Sir Henry. But Manfred closed his eyes with a groan. "Well," he thought; "here is an end to it."

Ponderer now started to trot toward the dragon, while Sir Henry pulled at the reins, without effect. However, the dragon had been taking deep breaths, and was now swollen to twice its size, and emitting dense clouds of smoke and flame; and this so frightened the horse that he stopped of his own accord, and backed rapidly away. This in turn surprised and disappointed the dragon. "Come, come," it protested; "I can't hold this pose forever." But the rapid forward and backward motion proved even more disconcerting to Sir Henry, who fell, in fact, into a kind of swoon, or syncope, and thus was carried forward once more toward the dragon, who opened his mouth to receive him.

This open mouth, ringed around with shining teeth, caused Ponderer to stop short again; which, in turn, caused Sir Henry's spear to topple forward from its carrying perch; the spear, falling with its point out beyond the horse's nose, dealt the animal a sharp rap on its neck as it fell, which made him give a convulsive jump forward; and the dragon, not expecting anything, received the point of the spear down its throat, exactly like the pictures of St. George. The air then immediately fled out of the beast with a loud report, the frightened horse jumped backwards, leaving the spear in the dragon's throat, and Sir Henry tumbled forward over the crupper, and landed on top of the dragon, which, bending upon him its dying glance, observed in tones of reproach: "You have killed me."

"In fair combat," murmured Sir Henry weakly.

"What was fair about it?" demanded the dragon indignantly.

Sir Henry rose unsteadily to his feet, and went in search of his sword. It was true that luck had played a part in the affair, but he did not feel like discussing it. He turned back to where Ponderer stood quietly waiting; and the Lady Alisane stepped out of the cave, dressed in her best kerchief, and carrying a basket on her arm.

"I thought you might want your tea," she said, "now that the fight is over."

. . . and by the dragon's ward

FOR tea, there were scones and marmalade, crumpets, honey, and small patties of some kind of meat. Sir Henry, with the dead dragon lying there in front of him, was a little doubtful of the meat, and managed to pass the patties on to Manfred without Alisane noticing. But the scones were good, warm and buttery; and Sir Henry felt quite peaceful, rested and comfortable.

Then, too, Alisane did not appear to be disturbed by the outcome of the battle, but seemed to have accepted her fate, or destiny, with cheerful indifference. And as she buttered a crumpet, before passing it to Sir Henry, she remarked:

"I'm glad that things turned out as they did; for I should dislike to be married to too much of a hero."

"Married?" said Sir Henry, looking a little startled.

"Why yes," said Alisane. And she added, with a smile:

"You are a lucky man."

Sir Henry stopped chewing, and stared at her in astonishment. "Me?" he said.

"The minute I saw you fall off your horse," said Alisane, "I thought to myself: that man is lucky. And that's so much better than mere strength of arms. To have luck, I mean. . . .

"I thought of something else, too," she went on. "I thought you ought to stay home more.

"Because you don't have a very good seat," she concluded, "and some day you might fall off again."

"I'm quite used to it," said Sir Henry. "But thank you, just the same."

"I don't think I should like to see my husband," said Alisane, "carried home on a stretcher very often."

"I have never considered myself particularly lucky," said Sir Henry.

Alisane hesitated for a moment. Then she said, all in a rush of breath: "I too must tell you something. I have no dowry."

"Well, there you are," said Sir Henry. And he added heavily: "I should have thought the dragon would have left you something."

"I thought you'd be pleased," said Alisane shyly. "This way, you'll be able to give me everything."

"Me?" said Sir Henry. "I?"

"I don't need very much, really," said Alisane. "I haven't many wants. I need a new kirtle, and a linen smock. And a cloak for the winter; and I should like some soft shoes, and stockings of silk. And some nice underthings. And a flagon of fragrance; and some red for my cheeks. And my own little cup of silver, with Alisane written on it, in letters.

"That's all," she said. "It's very little, really."

Sir Henry put a drop of honey on a scone, and then scraped it off again with his dagger. "To tell you the truth," he said, "I am scarcely in a position to support a wife."

"Oh," said Alisane. She looked at him for a moment; and then she looked away; and he could see that her chin trembled. "In that case," she said, "my poverty stands me in bad stead.

"But give me leave," she went on piteously, "to think myself in some kind of relation to you, if only a sister, or a cousin-german. For a name is all a woman has in this world, for better or worse; and while it is true that I lived with the dragon, it was as his ward, which in itself gave me a certain position; but now that he is slain I am truly alone, and most vulnerable."

And she did, indeed, at that moment look very small and defenseless in the world; and Sir Henry's heart hurt him. "What manner of man am I?" he thought. "This is unknightly of me.

"My dear," he said unhappily, "I have no practice in the art of marriage. I should make you a poor husband; and would be a sorry figure at a wedding, in my old clothes."

"It needn't be a real wedding," said Alisane eagerly, "in a cathedral . . . with the bells all ringing, and the choirboys singing. Actually, you have to have a cathedral for that, and you ought to have the parents of the bride; and I don't know where there's a cathedral, and I'm not at all sure where my parents are. But wherever they are, they'd be a lot happier, thinking me married. Or at least engaged."

"Yes, of course," said Sir Henry; "so they would. "There's no doubt about it."

"So you see," said Alisane.

Sir Henry sat very still for a moment, looking down at his hands. "Well," he thought, "there it is: One goes about one's business, one does one's duty, one does what is expected—and suddenly you're somebody's husband.

"I suppose we could go through some simple sort of ceremony," he said at last, "though it would scarcely be binding in the hereafter." "I will take my chances with the hereafter," said Alisane, "just so long as I need not be ashamed of my title to the present." "Well then," said Sir Henry with a sigh, "if you wish to consider yourself engaged, why so you may; and after a while we will say that we are married."

He felt rather surprised. He had been alone all his life, and now he was not going to be alone any more. It was a strange thing; he was not quite sure how he felt about it.

The dusk came down; the dark trees grew darker still, the shadowy air grew cold. A late bird sang; and the last bees went blundering home. The clear green lamp of evening was lit above them in the sky.

"Come," he said. "It is time to go in."

in which plans are made, heroism is discussed, and

a rabbit is outraged

ALISANE would have been content to settle down in the cave, which she insisted was perfectly comfortable; it was dry and roomy, and cool in summer and warm in winter. "I like my own bed," she declared, "and my little shelf; and after all, one does have memories of one's childhood home." "No," said Sir Henry, "for there are better places elsewhere; and I mean to find one for my wife." "Shall we be married soon?" asked Alisane. "Let us find a house first," said Sir Henry.

So the next morning they set off from the cave;

Alisane seated behind Sir Henry, and with her arms clasped around his middle, and Manfred trotting on ahead, and exploring the many interesting trees and bushes which bordered the forest path. At noon, being alongside of Indal Water, where it became Betcombe Mere, they stopped for lunch, which Alisane had thoughtfully provided from the dragon's larder. This time Sir Henry was sufficiently rested, and hungry enough to try the meat patties, which he found excellent, though he thought he would not ask Alisane what they were composed of. Manfred, having treed a squirrel, set up a great din, and had to be called in and silenced; after which they set out again, across the forest floor.

It was indeed, being early summer, a time for lovers; birds sang, the woods smelled sweet, and the open glades, bright with sun, were gay with butterflies. Leaves cast their dapple of shadow across the travelers, and Indal Water, on its way to being Malvern Stream, murmured below them, now green and silver at their feet, now lost to sight among the trees.

"My love," said Alisane, "I shall be sore tonight from sitting so long upon a horse."

"I have been thinking of that," said Sir Henry, "and although I do not see what can be done about it now, I do have in mind a little chaise, on two wheels, which we might engage to have built for us, and which I could attach in some manner to my charger's rear, and in which you could sit and take your ease."

"No woman ever had a better husband," said Alisane gratefully. "Let us hurry and find a wagon-maker or a wheelwright."

And she added: "I should like the interior to be lined with cherry-colored silk, with tassels of gold; and with a place for my brushes, and my long-handled mirror."

"I was not thinking about a lining for it," said Sir Henry.

That night he built her a shelter of hemlock boughs, over a bed of balsam, and they fell asleep in the cool still night, under Sir Henry's cloak. She lay with her cheek against his hand, and her lips slightly parted. Sir Henry, touched by her appearance, which was that of an innocent and trusting child, exclaimed in moving tones:

"I shall try to make her happy, and to be everything that she desires."

Alisane, who was not asleep, smiled comfortably to herself.

Her sleep was sweet, and unbroken; as she turned from time to time, she managed to wrap Sir Henry's cloak around her, leaving him uncovered, in his underwear.

In the morning they continued their journey, and had gentle discourse, and spoke amiably together, while Manfred addressed his friend Ponderer as follows:

"One goes upon many journeys in this life; and in the end, they are all part of the same pilgrimage. It is the pilgrimage of every living thing, of knights

and ladies, horses and dogs, ants, bees, and bee-
tles, as they pass from morning through noon to
night, from life to death. But no one knows the
character of the inn at which he will finally arrive,
or the nature of his rest there; or whether there
will be refreshment of any kind. This would naturally tend to make one want to slow up a little,
if it were possible; but it is not. And what unexpected accidents there are along the way!" "I
shall look ridiculous pulling a chaise," said Ponderer.

"One must not think too much about appear-
ances," said Manfred. "That is what caused the
trouble between Tristram and Yseult." "I do not
follow you," said Ponderer. "They were taken in
what appeared to be flagrante delicto," said Manfred, "and it was only afterwards that it was discovered that they were suffering from the effects of
drink." "I believe they both died of it," said Ponderer. "That is the story as it is usually told," replied the hound, "but the truth is, they became a

sort of public trust, and were married, and went to live in Kareol." "Ah," said Ponderer; "I hadn't heard. Now there's a happy ending! And did they love each other forever and ever?" "Only when drinking," said Manfred; "that is the sad part of it.

"So you can see, a chaise is not so bad; there are worse things." "You are not a horse," said Ponderer.

"My love," remarked Sir Henry to the Lady Alisane, "this landscape through which we are passing is not more gentle than your own nature, such as I have observed it to be in these few hours that I have known you." "Thank you," replied Alisane; "but I am not really gentle, and can be like a shrew at times."

"It is the nature of a woman to be gentle," said Sir Henry; "whereas, in a knight, it would be a fault. For he must first win his spurs; and later, his livelihood, and he is not likely to succeed at either, by gentle means." "That is where a woman can do wonders to help," said Alisane. "Do you think so?"

asked Sir Henry. "I am sure of it," said Alisane.

There were no further adventures that day; no one stopped them, and no one spoke to them. At evening, coming to a small chapel among the trees, they alighted, and went in to make their orisons; after which the Lady Alisane, looking around her, remarked: "Why not rest here for the night, in good shelter from the damps, and out of reach of evil spirits or sorcerers?" To which Sir Henry replied that for the two of them to sleep together in a church would be an impious and profane act. "I would agree with you," said Alisane, "if we were married; but we are not. And you would be right, perhaps, if we were not married; . . . but after all, although we are not, we do intend to be, and are in a most fragrant state of grace, which is to be affianced but not wed, and without quarrels or disagreements."

Sir Henry sighed. "A chapel is a mournful place, particularly at night," he said; "it is full of reminders of man's destiny." "It is a reminder of heaven," said Alisane, "and I am surprised that you should have forgotten it." "I did not exactly forget it," said Sir Henry.

"It was in a chapel like this," he said, "that I watched over my armor on the occasion of my initiation into knighthood. I was young, and filled with ambition; my dreams stood about me like angels with folded wings. Galahad, Lancelot . . . I meant to outdo them all, in honor and courage; with my sword and spear, I intended to carve a career for myself that would echo through history. I have felt a little melancholy about chapels ever since; for I have collected little more than rust on my journey." "Thank you," said Alisane coldly. "Thank you very much." "I was not speaking of you," said Sir Henry; and he added hopefully:

"I had in mind a certain haystack for the night, such as we passed awhile back."

"No, thank you," said Alisane; "I should be swollen-eyed in the morning, from sneezing all night. However," she added, "you have reminded me that we did pass a small farm of some sort, with a garden; and if you will go back and pick me a few lettuces, I will make you a salad for your supper." "Well," began Sir Henry doubtfully. . . . "We also—now that I think of it," continued Alisane, "passed a cherry tree, hung with ripe fruit; bring me a few red cherries, for there is nothing better to dress a salad than cherries or grapes." "Well, there you are," said Manfred to himself. "Absent thee from felicity awhile."

Sir Henry went back to the garden, and pulled up half a score of lettuces, and, with a few cherries, returned to the chapel, where Alisane had already made a sauce or dressing for her salad, of vinegar and oil, bay, mustard, tansy, and wild carrot. The lettuces being then washed, and the sauce and cherries set on top, they commenced their supper seated on the steps of the chapel, while the dusk came down. When they were finished, Sir Henry took Alisane gently by the hand, and remarked:

"Let me look at you, because I forget sometimes, during the day, how pretty you look."

Alisane blushed with surprise and pleasure, and immediately took her hand away, to smooth her hair. "It is because you do not see me," she said, "sitting as I do behind you all day on the horse."

"Would you rather sit before me?" asked Sir Henry.

"I would like a little chaise," said Alisane, "with a lining of cherry silk."

A little while later, she murmured:

"Do not be impatient, I am still very young."

"I love your being young," said Sir Henry.

"Yet you," mused Alisane, "are somewhat grizzled with age."

"That is why I wear your youth like a favor," said Sir Henry simply.

"I see," said Alisane. "That was rather sweet."

And she added in a conversational voice:

"When do you think we will be married?"

"Presently," said Sir Henry.

A rabbit and his wife, on their way home to their

burrow, stopped a moment and sniffed the air. "Someone has been having a salad here," said the rabbit. "What a feast."

The doe's nose twitched, for she smelled the salad dressing. "Things are not simple any more," she declared. "We have lost our simplicity in this country."

in which Sir Henry and the Lady Alisane stop for tea

with a sorcerer

SIR HENRY and Alisane traveled for several days in good company with each other; and came finally to the Wastes of Ende, where the sorcerer Alyot had his castle. As our travelers left the shade of the forest, and emerged into meadow land, a sweet humming or singing filled the air around them, as if it were plucked from the strings of harps, the wings of bees, and the throats of birds; while a choir of boy sopranos, or so it seemed, intoned a Jubilate in the Lydian mode. Yet neither birds nor bees were to be seen, either among the grasses or the trees; nor were the boy sopranos visible, or their concert place apparent.

As they approached the castle, which appeared to be a small one, but surrounded by flowers of the loveliest hues, a train of ladies and gentlemen rode out to greet them, which, upon coming nearer, were seen to be richly dressed, and of a courteous bearing, all of them smiling welcome, and waving garlands. Sir Henry, turning to his lady to express his opinion of this, found her staring open-mouthed before her, and giving expression to little cries of delight; at which, turning back in surprise, he found the company of ladies and gentlemen vanished, and in their place a panoply of birds in bright plumage, and a sport of lambs at play.

Moving through these flocks and herds, which seemed to flow about them, only to vanish and re-appear again at a distance, Sir Henry and the Lady Alisane approached the castle, which they now saw to be made entirely of glass, but so cunningly contrived that while one wall afforded a view of the interior, the other threw back to the traveler his own startled face, complete with landscape; in this way, the castle itself appeared to be of different sizes, and, as it were, of uncertain actuality, now there and now not.

The drawbridge being lowered, our two travelers, along with Manfred, traversed the moat at a smart trot, and dismounted in a small courtyard, where they were immediately waited upon by a proper groom and a young page, and were invited upstairs into the presence of Alyot himself.

They found the sorcerer in his tower room, which contained a library of some size, consisting of parchments, papyri, tablets, and churchly histories in oaken covers, as well as certain chronicles in Hebrew, Langue d'oc, Sanskrit, and Greek. Upon Alyot's welcoming the travelers by name, at which Alisane could not conceal her surprise, the sorcerer declared that he was familiar with Sir Henry's travels, and had been for some time.

"I know everything," he said quietly. "I know the names of all knights, and their ladies, and their condition and degree; also all dragons, ogres, kings, and commonalty. I am analytic in temper, and of catholic mind, which of itself creates a sufficient dichotomy; my two selves, uniting and separating, furnish and nourish the tides of my spirit, from which rise bubbles of fancy such as you find in soda water, and also a very adequate magic, slightly dry." "I did so like the birds and the singing," said Alisane.

"Thank you," said Alyot; "I think that first impressions are so important. What has been seen, for the first time, in loveliness or splendor, will always have something splendid or lovely about it. You, dear Lady Alisane, will always appear to me the way I saw you first, trotting across the draw-bridge, the very picture of happiness, seated upon the rear end of a horse." "Sir Henry is going to get me a little chaise," said Alisane. "I would be only too happy to provide it myself," said Alyot with a bow, "but I'm afraid in the end you would find it was made out of a pumpkin." "Still," said Alisane doubtfully, "if it had the appearance of a chaise . . ." "Why so it would," replied Alyot, "but the mice would be at it." He continued:

"All of us, in this world, lead lives half way between what is and what is not—with dream and fact balanced upon either end of a pole like a teeterer on a stretched wire. Some lean to wishfulness, and some to the other side, and the truth, perhaps, is between; but hidden. For there is nothing but appearance, to our eyes; and so, illusion; and therefore, fraud."

"It is a sad thought to think," said Alisane, "for it makes one feel uncertain."

"Uncertainty too," said Alyot, gazing at her with light green eyes, "is illusion; and illusion is still magic. In particular, that illusion between a man and a woman, which we call love; and which is actually a taking, or spell, with malaise and fever, and other symptoms of the heart.

"If one has a heart," he added.

Alyot turned toward a side-table, and taking up a small crystal goblet, filled it with liquid from a silver flask, and offered it to Alisane. "Allow me," he said; "this little wine from our own grapes, which have been called foxy by some, but they were envious when they said so."

When Alisane hesitated to accept the goblet, Alyot smiled. "Are you afraid of me?" he asked. "Why," said Alisane, "what an idea."

"I do not mind if you are afraid of me," said Alyot. "It means that you will not forget me right away."

"Oh," said Alisane; "do you think not?" And she shook her curls archly.

"I think not," said Alyot, smiling.

Alisane took the goblet, and drained it; but her hand trembled a little. "What made you think I was afraid of you?" she said boldly, looking Alyot full in the face. But after a moment she bit her lip and looked away. "I am not frightened," said

Alisane, "but my heart belongs to Sir Henry.

"And that is strange too, I think," she added, "because we are not married yet."

"You are very young," said Alyot, "and I am envious of Sir Henry. I can remember when I, too, was young; and little girls were all beautiful and good. And also secret, strange, troubling, and desirable. I used to imagine that some day I would die, quietly and sweetly, with my head in a little girl's lap. I was myself so small at the time, it is a miracle I survived." "It is indeed," agreed Sir Henry, "for if you are not clever with a sword or a battle axe, your chances are not very good." "We are to be married presently," said Alisane.

"And yet," said Alyot, "I did survive; I created an illusion of strength, and in this I sat, not unlike a sapsucker in its bubble-bath, secure from everyone except my imitators. For I found that I had set a fashion; and that many young sorcerers had followed my example. Without my knowledge, and lacking my wit, their bubbles turned out to be dull affairs, and never shone like mine."

"Then is this castle an illusion?" asked Sir Henry in surprise.

"It is indeed," replied Alyot, "and rises, from the Wastes of Ende, and from the nightingales, into the most catholic mysteries where there are no songs of nightingales at all. There all is peace . . . except for certain theological problems. And perhaps—" he sighed— "a certain emptiness . . . of heart. . . ."

"I do not like to think that your heart is empty," said Alisane.

"Perhaps it need not be," said Alyot.

The sorcerer drew Alisane away into a small tire-room, off to one side. "Pardon me," he said to Sir Henry; "I have something to say to your lady."

"Well . . ." said Sir Henry.

Alyot closed the door behind himself and Alisane, and Sir Henry set himself to wait. "I cannot imagine what he can have to say to Alisane," he thought, "because she is not particularly clever or

even very well educated." But presently he found
that he was clasping and unclasping his hands, and
that he had a heavy feeling in his stomach. As the
moments passed, and neither Alisane nor Alyot reappeared, Sir Henry began to perspire; he felt
quite miserable, and told himself that he had been
poisoned. "Make my bed soon," he exclaimed,
"for I'm sick to my heart, and I fain would lie
down."

The hound, Manfred, lying at his feet, was half
asleep, when a household mouse approached him,
and courteously inquired if he was enjoying himself. "Well," replied Manfred with a yawn, "I have
had better times. What is your name, if I
may ask?"

"Wondermeier," said the mouse.

"In that case, Wondermeier," said Manfred, "I
wonder if you could lead me to the kitchen, where,
with luck, I might find a bone or two, or even some
scraps; for I have not yet had anything to eat."

The mouse smiled sadly. "I could lead you to

the kitchen," he said, "but you would not find anything there. Our food, like everything else, is an
illusion; and the master is now working on a
scheme to make our appetites equally illusory."
"Your master," said Manfred idly, "is working at
something entirely different." But Wondermeier
shook his head. "That is what you think," he said.

And taking Manfred by the paw, he led him
over to a crack in the door, and bade him look.

"It is the master spell," said Wondermeier, "by
which he enchants even himself . . . for a little
while. And then it always turns out the same way
—badly; because he has never been able to fool
himself long enough."

"Do you mean that love is an illusion?" cried
Manfred, "even to Alyot?"

"Even to Alyot," replied Wondermeier.

Manfred gazed through the crack in the door,
and saw Alyot plain; the sorcerer sat alone, his
head bowed upon his chest, and his cheeks wet
with lonely tears.

vi

in which Sir Henry adds somewhat embarrassingly

to his entourage

SIR HENRY and Lady Alisane left the sorcerer's castle, crossing the same flowery moat and blossoming meadows as before, and after that finding themselves in open country, given mostly to pasture. For a long time they were quiet; Sir Henry was taken with the expression on Alisane's face, which was one of hurt surprise.

"It was a pretty castle," he said at last, "but I had a feeling that it was not very solid."

Alisane did not reply. Her eyes seemed to be focused on some unknown shore, mysterious and distant. After a while she roused herself; and a light sigh escaped her.

"Do you not think so, my love?" asked Sir Henry.

Alisane looked at him in a puzzled way. "Think what?" she asked.

"Why," said Sir Henry, "it's all very well to make people think they see flowers where they don't, but a glass house is not very strong against assault."

"Don't be too sure," said Alisane. A moment later, she added:

"How does one arm oneself against beauty?"

When Sir Henry did not reply, having no answer to that, she added, almost to herself:

"So to be taken by surprise!"

"It was an illusion," said Sir Henry heavily. "It was a spell."

"It was an illusion," she agreed. "And yet my heart was plucked by magic, and to my sorrow."

"To mine also," said Sir Henry. "I wonder that

so much was made of it," said Alisane brightly, "for in the morning light, it seems a trifle." "Why, so it was, my dear," said Sir Henry, "but I think that we will put off our marriage for a little."

At this Alisane began to weep silently. Sir Henry said nothing to comfort her; and she presently dried her eyes, and remarked in quiet tones:

"Perhaps you would like to be rid of me altogether."

"Certainly not," said Sir Henry. "It would be an unknightly thing to do."

"Is that the only reason?" asked Alisane piteously.

"No," said Sir Henry.

"I'm glad of that," she said; and waited for Sir Henry to say something more. But Sir Henry said nothing; and they continued on their way in silence.

In the late afternoon, as they came out of the woods into a green meadow, they saw a strange knight approaching from the opposite direction, also with a lady upon his pillion, who called upon Sir Henry to stand and declare himself. "Why then," said Sir Henry, reining in his charger, "I am Henry of Brentwood; and this is my Lady, Alisane. We have lately come from the castle of Alyot, the sorcerer; and mean to continue, if you will be so kind as to step aside to let us pass." "Not in a thousand years," said the strange knight, "for I have made a vow to let no one pass me." "A stupid vow," declared Sir Henry, "for in that case you must find yourself at cross purposes with everyone you meet." "So I must," replied the knight. "And do you enjoy it?" asked Sir Henry. "It is a living," said the knight.

Sir Henry helped Alisane to alight. "I am sorry, my dear," he said with a sigh, "but there is no help for it. This fellow means to have at me, for which reason I must have at him; and so forth." "What happens if you lose?" asked Alisane anxiously. "Why then he will have you as prize," replied Sir

Henry, "along with my armor, and Ponderer." "And if you win?" asked Alisane; "what then?" "Then," said Sir Henry, "I shall have whatever is his." "And will you have his lady also?" asked Alisane. "Why yes," said Sir Henry, "I suppose so." "That could be very awkward," said the Lady Alisane. "I cannot very well help it," said Sir Henry.

Sir Henry laid his spear in rest; but before he began his charge, he addressed a few words to his horse, Ponderer. "Please do not stop," he said, "before you get there; close your eyes if you must, but go briskly forward to whatever glory awaits us." "That's all very well," remarked Ponderer to Manfred, "but I do not think anything awaits us except a nasty jolt." "It is much worse for me," replied Manfred, "who have to watch it."

Sir Henry shook the reins of his charger; and the strange knight and he approached each other at a smart canter, Sir Henry's spear centered upon his foe's shield, the stranger's aimed at Sir Henry's visor, which was generally conceded to be the better objective, and showed a superior technique. However, at that moment Alisane choosing to hurl the word Philanderer after him, Sir Henry turned his head to admonish her, and both spears missing their objective, the two knights were carried past each other without hurt, and disappeared into the woods at opposite ends of the meadow.

A few minutes later they reappeared again, and took up their positions facing each other. But now the strange knight was on the side nearest Alisane, and Sir Henry found himself close to the stranger's lady. "What is your name, my dear?" he asked.

The damsel dropped him a curtsy. "Meghan," she said, with a friendly smile.

She was, Sir Henry was glad to see, an attractive young lady. "Well then, Meghan," he said, "if I win you, you will have to go with me." "Where to?" she asked. When Sir Henry replied that he didn't know, she looked surprised. "A man must know where he is going," she said, "but if you

are upon a quest, I will go with you right willingly." "Well," said Sir Henry uncertainly, "I suppose I do have my mind set upon something." "Is
it the Grail?" asked Meghan eagerly. "Well, no,"
said Sir Henry; "not exactly. I had not thought to
reach so far."

The damsel's face fell. "There is nothing like
the Grail," she said, "to move a man to heroic
deeds." But in a moment she brightened up again.
"Still in all," she declared, "there are other good
quests, for the spirit's sake." "Well," said Sir
Henry, "I do not have any name for my quest; but
we are going to Tintagel, if that suit you." "I do
not mind where we go," said Meghan, "as long as
it is for honor and renown."

Sir Henry and the stranger now set heels to
their chargers again, and meeting this time in full
career, unhorsed each other, and fell flat upon
their backs on the earth. The fall loosed Sir Henry's helmet, which, on his scrambling to his feet,
fell off, leaving him unhelmed, and at a disadvan-

tage. Seeing this, the stranger stepped back, and asked him if he would yield; to which Sir Henry, shaken by his fall, and not hearing what he said, merely shook his head, to clear the fog away.

"As you please," said the stranger, and aimed a sharp blow with his sword at Sir Henry's head. Being bareheaded, Sir Henry could easily see it coming, and was able to duck out of the way; and, in turn, gave the stranger a resounding clout with his sword, which rang so many gongs inside the stranger's helmet that he was all but deafened. His return blow caught Sir Henry's shield, and the two knights continued then to exchange buffets with swords which had long ago been pounded to the point of dullness upon other people's armor.

Presently, by mutual agreement, they stopped to rest, and sat down together under a tree in the shade, while their ladies waited upon them, Alisane on Sir Henry, and Meghan on the stranger. Alisane brought forth the remains of the salad, and some cheese; and Meghan contributed some slices of bread and a stoup of wine; and the four of them rested, and feasted together in good company. "It is too bad that we cannot join forces," said the stranger, "and go on together; it would be pleasant for the ladies to have someone to talk to, and you and I could practice feats of arms, and keep each other company in the evenings." "I could not agree with you more," said Sir Henry, "and suggest that you turn back, and ride with us in the direction in which we are going." "I have just come from there," said the stranger, "but do you turn back, and go my way with me." "That is impossible," said Sir Henry, "because I am going in the opposite direction." "Well, then," said the strange knight, "there is no help for it, we must fight it out." "It seems almost too bad," said Sir Henry.

"Excuse me a moment," said Alisane to the others; and leaning over, whispered something in Sir Henry's ear. Sir Henry looked startled.

"It would be unfair," he said.

"And if you have your head hacked off," she asked, "what then?"

"Well . . ." said Sir Henry uncomfortably.

"A woman should help all she can," said Alisane.

"I wonder if I might ask a favor of you," said the strange knight. "I noticed that you fought without your helmet; and it seemed to give you rather an advantage in mobility, and so forth; would you mind if I did the same?" "Not at all," said Sir Henry; "suit yourself."

The two knights prepared to resume their battle; when Alisane, suddenly running over to the Lady Meghan, dealt her a buffet across the ears which brought her down flat upon her back. At Meghan's cry of dolor, the strange knight stopped in surprise, and looked around in time to see his lady rise and deal Alisane a buffet in turn, which brought her to her knees. "Well done," cried the knight. "A shrewd blow."

A moment later, seeing the Lady Meghan again stretched out upon the turf, he exclaimed:

"Oh, I say."

At this moment, while the knight's attention was on his lady's battle, Sir Henry took his sword and dealt him a great clout on the head, which split it open.

The strange knight fell upon the grass. Meghan went to him, and dutifully took his broken head upon her lap; at which, looking up at Sir Henry, he declared feebly:

"That was most unfair of you. Now I leave you, as is the custom, my belongings: my horse, my feather bed, or quilt, my armor, and my lady. The armor has served me well; if I had only worn it, I should not be in my present case. My lady's name is Meghan. . . ."

"I know," said Sir Henry.

The dying man rested for a moment, gathering his strength. "She is not at all what you might expect," he said at last. "Her father was Preceptor of Dorchester, and she is widely traveled. At sixteen she went to habit with a clerk who was then at work on The Little Commentary, and left him because he failed to move up to The Greater Commentary. She is ambitious; and had great hopes for me."

And he added with a feeble sigh:

"She will make a hero of you, if she can."

Alisane, whose ears were still ringing from the blows, exclaimed:

"I have other plans for my husband."

"Then I am sorry for you," whispered the stranger; and soon was dead.

Sir Henry, feeling somewhat moved by all this, blew his nose; but a moment later, uttered an exclamation of dismay.

"I have the nosebleed," he declared.

CHAPTER

vii

wherein we are introduced to several different points

of view

"WHAT is your name?" asked Ponderer politely,
as the two horses moved side by side across the
meadowy turf. Sir Henry and Alisane rode seated
on Ponderer as before; while Lady Meghan rode
her own, except that now she rode in the saddle,
while her late champion's armor and personal belongings were piled on the pillion. She was quiet,
and seemed to be in fair spirits.

"Simpkins," said the horse.

"I hope that you will be happy with us," said
Ponderer.

Simpkins looked at him in surprise. "Happy?" he asked. "What is happy about being a horse? One works; and eats—perhaps; and sleeps when and where one can. One trots about in the broiling sun, or stands for hours in the freezing rain; and once a month or so one finds oneself in the middle of a sanguinary battle, charging about, here and there, left and right. The work is arduous, and the rewards are few." "Still," said Ponderer, "you do not have to stay awake nights trying to save humanity." "If you ask me," said Simpkins, "humanity does not want to be saved at all.

"That is to say," he added, "that everybody would like to be saved by himself, with his damsel and his feather bed and maybe a cousin or two, but no one cares about saving humanity in general, by which I mean all the rest of the people."

To this Manfred, who was trotting along beside them, replied:

"One is either a hero, or an ant. Among heroes I list the birds of prey, the falcons, eagles, and bustards, the larger fish of the sea such as the shark, octopus, and sea serpent, the dragon, the gryphon, and man; for each thinks first and only of himself, and would destroy those like himself for a meal or an advantage. Whereas an ant thinks first and only of his fellow ants." "There have been no love poems written by ants," said Simpkins.

"It is quite a problem," said Manfred, "to choose between mankind and the hymenoptera. The ant's life is laid out for him; his duties are clear, and he is not given enough liberty to get him into trouble. All his needs are taken care of; he is fed and housed at the expense of the community. Unlike man, he does not enjoy a tendency to commit suicide. He is strong and lively, and his armor is built to measure." "An ant is a rough-and-tumble fighter," said Ponderer, "but lacks finesse."

"He does not drag himself through his old age," said Manfred, "rheumy and full of pain. Has one ever seen an ant with the gout? When he can no longer work, he is bitten in two, and used in the kitchen. Nothing is wasted; everything is dedicated."

"It appears to me," said Simpkins to Ponderer, "that our friend here would rather be an ant than a hero." "What?" cried Manfred; "and give up my right to the life of a dog? To the fresh smells of morning, the warm fragrances of noon, the hunt, the chase, the aroma of cooking, the sweetness of bones, the delight of the moonlight, the terror of death, and the behinds of my friends? Never! Not in a thousand years." "There it is," said Simpkins; "each to his own."

Meanwhile, above them the following conversation was taking place:

"I am sorry that I was obliged to box your ears," said Alisane to Meghan, "but if I had not made a diversion, Sir Henry might have been slain. However, now that it is over, I hope that you will be comfortable with us; and you must be sure to tell me if you want something or if there is anything lacking." "Why so I will, and thank you," said

Meghan. "Though I do not suppose you have a lute." "No," said Alisane, "I am not musical." "That is too bad," said Meghan; "I am very musical, but sing only with accompaniment." "What a pity," said Alisane.

"You understand," she said gently, a short while later, "that Sir Henry will expect to use your late companion's feather bed, or puff." "He is welcome to it," said Meghan, "for it's warm in the middle, and cold at the ends, as I've discovered."

"It is the same thing with the seasons of the year," said Sir Henry, "for they start in January and end in December, with the summer in between." "As for me," said Meghan, "I like the springtime best."

Later, as they rested for the night under a great tree, Meghan remarked:

"I was not married to the knight you killed, nor, for that matter, much taken with him. And as long as you go in search of honor and glory, I am well satisfied to go with you; though for that matter

I have little other choice now except to enter a convent." To which Alisane replied shortly: "Our quest is for a small castle, with a moat; and for a fortune, and the enjoyment of it."

"That is not very heroic," said Meghan. "I would not wish to be the wife of a fief-holder."

"King Arthur was a fief-holder," said Alisane. "And no one asked you to be anybody's wife."

"He was not as great a hero," said Meghan stoutly, "as Sir Perceval, that sought the Grail."

"Still and all," said Sir Henry, sticking his head out from under the feather bed, "it is the man who must make a living, and the headaches and broken bones are his."

"I was only thinking of what was best for you," said Meghan humbly. "Oh?" said Alisane quietly; "and is there anything better for a man than a home?" "Why, yes," said Meghan; "a high heart is better."

"Well," said Sir Henry peevishly, "you are keeping me awake; and I do not know which is better, anyway."

So saying, he put his head back under the puff again, and was soon asleep.

In the morning, they resumed their journey, over the blossoming earth, Meghan merrily greeting all they passed, whether of high or low degree, for she was a friendly girl, and wished everyone well. The air was fresh and clear, and the sky as blue as water, upon which sailed an armada of snowy clouds. "There is a tale," said Meghan, "that there are endless waters to the west, culminating in the great maw of Leviathan himself, in front of which rages a whirlpool beyond any imagining and so the end of all. While others believe that there are countries there, filled with monsters and cockatrices, which, to subdue, it is only necessary to cross the western ocean." "There are enough cockatrices at home," said Alisane.

Sir Henry felt quite happy. The breeze blew

sweetly through Meghan's pretty curls and Alisane's kerchief, the sun sparkled upon Sir Henry's armor, and the birds sang. One of them addressed himself to Manfred.

"Do not believe that the earth is flat," he said, "for it is as round as an egg. You have only to fly in one direction long enough, to find yourself back where you started from."

"There is no progress there," said Manfred. "It is of no benefit to anyone."

Sir Henry turned to Meghan. "Tell me again," he said, "of those far-off lands across the sea; and tell me where I may find the high heart to take me through the world with only a sword and a feather bed." "Why, you need only look within your ribs for it," said Meghan, "and below the collarbone." "I fear there is an empty space," said Alisane, "and all illusion."

in which our travelers reach the city of Chichester

Now for a few days a fog set in, and Sir Henry discovering a dry cave, they set up housekeeping in it, at which Alisane felt quite at home, but Meghan found herself more uncomfortable. Still, they were dry, and warm; for Sir Henry had made a good fire near the cave entrance, which caused at least some of the smoke to go outside; and Alisane took out her bone needle and her thread, to mend Sir Henry's underwear. "I do not understand why you have so many holes," she said, "unless it is moths; or do you wear your underwear into battle?" "I do not always have time to take it off,"

Sir Henry admitted; "and besides, I have had it now these several years." "It should be washed more often," said Alisane; "I must purchase some lye at the nearest town, to make a leach." "I'm afraid it will shrink," said Sir Henry.

While Alisane mended, Meghan practiced on the bow and arrow against Sir Henry's feather bed. "Be careful not to tear holes in it," said Sir Henry, "for I consider it an unusual and valuable piece." "Why not try your bow and arrow against a rabbit," said Alisane, "and see if you can feed us for a day or two?"

Sir Henry broomed the cave, with a broom of dry sticks; and brought in the firewood; but there were no rabbits to be found, and after two days of living on bread and cheese, our travelers were hungry. However, the fog fortunately lifting on the third day, they were able to proceed on their journey; and Meghan managing to knock over a squirrel, Alisane prepared it in a stew, not very palatable, but nourishing.

At the end of the fourth day, they came to the city of Chichester, at which Alisane was enchanted out of all speech, never having seen a city before of such size and magnificence, with its houses all of wood, its inn, its market place, and people in the streets. "Surely," she exclaimed, "this is the greatest city in the world!" But Meghan replied that she had been in greater cities, where there had been as many as a thousand persons at one time. "The world is getting crowded," said Sir Henry; "before long there will not be enough food for the population." "There is not enough now," said Manfred to himself.

The travelers put up at the inn, first arranging for the stabling of the two chargers; after which they supped very well upon a shoulder of mutton and a pasty of venison, several cups of sack each, and a jelly roll. The meal finished, the ladies arranged themselves upon a comfortable bed of straw under their own blankets, Sir Henry settled himself contentedly on the rushes of the floor with his feather bed on top of him, and Manfred went off into a corner with the mutton bone.

In the morning, after a hearty breakfast of sausage, pudding, cheese, and ale, Sir Henry went off to attend to his affairs, while the ladies, dressed in their best kerchiefs, went radiantly out to enjoy the sights of the city. "I have never heard so much noise in my life," said Alisane; "it would be enough to drive me out of my wits." "It is a fine place to visit," said Meghan, "but I would not want to live here." "I think I could grow used to it in time," said Alisane; "for there are so many interesting things to do.

"Even the air is different, in the city."

And it did, as a matter of fact, smell of many exciting and interesting things; of cook-stoves and peat fires, of open drains, of fresh-cut wood and spun flax, of boiled cabbages, and fresh bread, the warm breath of cattle, the sourness of wine, the dustiness of houses, and the sweetness of women.

Sir Henry went first to the smithy, to have his

sword sharpened, and found that he had to wait a short while in line before he could be attended to. When it came time for his repairs, he found that the price had been raised. "When were you last serviced?" asked the smith; and when Sir Henry replied that it had been a matter of two years or so, he shrugged his shoulders. "Well," he said, "there you are; the price of labor has gone up, spare bits and parts are hard to get, and we have to add the King's tax, and the Sheriff's tax." "I have a whole extra suit of armor I would like to sell," said Sir Henry; "if spare parts are in good demand and low supply, I should get a good price for it." "I buy whatever I need from the factor," replied the smith. "I will go to see him," said Sir Henry.

He found the factor in his warehouse, among bales of woolen cloth, bolts of silk, heaps of skins both furred and bare, and an assortment of rusty tools, implements, wooden plows, and iron mattocks. "Sir," said Sir Henry, "I have a good suit of armor—" But the factor stopped him before he could go any further. "I have more used armor," he said, "than I know what to do with."

Sir Henry stared at him in disbelief. "It was the smith himself who told me that armor was in short supply," he said.

The factor shrugged his shoulders. "There is always enough of everything," he said, "for those who can afford it. In fact, I can sell you a very fine morion this very moment, with only a small crack in it, which is scarcely even noticeable from the front." "I do not have a morion," said Sir Henry wistfully. "That will be two schillings," said the factor.

"I had also in mind to order a small chaise," said Sir Henry, "for one of my companions." "You will have to see the carriage-maker about that," said the factor. "Chaises are not in my line."

So Sir Henry went to see the carriage-maker, who listened to him with a careful air. "I can build you a chaise such as you describe," he said, "with two wheels; but have you considered the greater comfort you would enjoy from four?" "It's not for me," said Sir Henry, "but for a lady." "Ladies always prefer four wheels," said the carriage-maker, "for they make a better showing, and are more solid on the road."

And, in an easy tone, he added:

"It will be a little more expensive, but on the other hand, you will have a really first-class vehicle."

"How much more expensive would it be?" asked Sir Henry.

"About double," said the carriage-maker. "And a little extra for the lining."

That evening, when Sir Henry returned to the inn, the ladies each presented him with a gift. Alisane had bought him a stone hot-water-bottle, to place at his feet on cold nights, "because," she observed, "there is nothing to draw a man home like a warm bed, and no one is at his best with cold feet, however inclined." "I thank you for your thoughtfulness," said Sir Henry. "It is nothing," said Alisane; "I am obliged to be thoughtful under the circumstances."

Meghan brought her gift to him as he sat by the fire, and kneeling prettily in front of him, strapped it to his right heel. It was a single spur of fine design, and fashioned of silver; one spur being all, she explained, that she could afford. "You are very kind," said Sir Henry; "it will remind me of my quest." "That is what I thought," said Meghan. "What quest is that?" asked Alisane sharply. "I do not know yet," said Sir Henry. "But I think it is to the west."

"It is the spirit that matters," said Meghan, "not the name." "Then I do not see why you give him a spur," said Alisane, "for he will only hit his horse with it, or his own backside, and not his spirit at all."

"That is a very horrid remark," said Meghan, "and I would not have made it." "Well," said Alisane, "maybe not; but I did." "Then you have reason to be sorry," said Meghan. "I am not sorry at all," said Alisane.

Sir Henry then brought out gifts for each of them, which he had purchased in town. For Alisane he had a silver porringer, which gave her great satisfaction, because it had her name written on it in Gothic letters. "With this," she exclaimed, "I shall be able to start my housekeeping. It is our first piece of furniture; and I shall always treasure it." "It is a solid piece of silver," said Sir Henry, "and quite valuable."

For Meghan, he had an Irish lute, of delicate design, which made her first cry out in surprise and then weep a little. "I cannot think of anything I would rather have," she said, "and I will never be able to thank you enough." "Then let us have a little music," said Sir Henry; "strike up a melody, and accompany yourself on the lute; it should be very agreeable." "The trouble is," said Meghan, "I do not know how to play it.

"Yet," she added.

. . . and rest there in good comfort

IN THE next several days Sir Henry made a number of visits to the carriage shop, accompanied by his ladies. Meghan was soon bored, but Alisane liked nothing better than to sit quietly among the wood shavings and watch her coach take shape. She did not hesitate to make suggestions as the work progressed. "I don't believe the front and rear seats should face each other," she said, "since that tends to do away with privacy to any degree." "I am not interested in privacy," said the carriage-maker; "all I'm trying for is balance." "There is no balance in this situation," said Alisane simply.

"On the contrary," said Sir Henry, "it seems to me that I am very nicely balanced indeed." "With dream and fact," said Alisane, "at either end of a pole." "You took that from Alyot," said Sir Henry accusingly. "I did," said Alisane, "and I was sorry for him, for there was no one in the world more alone than he."

But the almost daily visit to the carriage shop was not the only activity in which our travelers engaged; for Meghan had found a teacher upon the lute, and was taking lessons upon that instrument; and Sir Henry was studying the higher school of the broadsword and dagger at the Fencing Academy, under the tutelage of an aged knight who had fought in France. "The French have many clever tricks," Sir Henry told Meghan, to whom he was explaining the riposte in tierce, and from the second position; "and as one grows older, and the joints are not as supple as they were, and the arms and legs grow a little rubbery . . ." "I wish you wouldn't talk like that," said Meghan;

"for you make me feel sorry for you, and then when I am not looking, you whack me."

But she nevertheless urged Sir Henry to try out several new steps, thrusts, and feints on her, and helped him courteously to his feet each time he fell down. "It is this heavy sword," he explained, "which throws me off balance."

"I know," said Meghan, "and it would be better for you if you hit me with it; then you wouldn't fall down." "No," said Sir Henry, "but you would." "I am glad you are so thoughtful of me," said Meghan; "you must like me a little."

"Must you and Meghan spend so much time thumping each other?" asked Alisane. "It can scarcely be pleasant for her." "She does me a lot of good," said Sir Henry, "for she encourages me to be more knightly." "That is very sweet of her," said Alisane darkly, "I am sure."

Alisane had made friends with the cook at the inn, with whom she spent long afternoons practicing her cooking, and learning new recipes. One in particular took her fancy, a recipe for a swivet stew, or stew of swivets. "It sounds divine," she explained to Meghan and Sir Henry. "It seems you take two swivets left over from lunch . . ." "What on earth is a swivet?" asked Sir Henry. "I don't know yet," said Alisane. "I think it is a kind of rabbit."

Meghan also spent some time in the offices of the Grey Brothers, or Traveling Friars, going over maps, routes, and travel itineraries. "We would be delighted to arrange a little tour for you," said the Brother in charge, "in any direction you like; for instance, there is a very lovely trip indeed, with stop-overs at Pevensey, Hastings, Dover, Calais, Arques, Ile of France, Limoges, Toulouse, Nice, Rome, Byzantium, Acre, and the Holy City itself, if you can get in." "Thank you," said Meghan; "I believe we are only going as far as Tintagel, but I love to think about such things."

She and Alisane attended a lecture by a poet, with readings and an accompaniment upon the flute; also a concert upon the recorder by a famous musician from Nottingham. The recorder enchanted them; "It has such a sweetly-sour sound," said Alisane; but they were disappointed in the poet, who had a ragged and unwashed appearance, and whose verses were entirely incomprehensible to them. "I am very fond of art," said Alisane, "and I like a bit of poetry now and then; but I prefer to know what it is all about." "I found that by closing my eyes," said Meghan, "and not thinking about anything, I did receive certain suggestions and images from the sound of the words." "What did you see, then, in your mind?" asked Alisane; "hills and valleys, and dancing shepherdesses?" "I saw three triangles," said Meghan, "and an egg."

Sir Henry and the ladies also went to a mime, held in the municipal gardens, in which they watched a knight slay a dragon made of paper, which vomited smoke. "Whoever wrote this piece," said Sir Henry gloomily, "knows nothing whatever about dragons, for this fellow is going at it with his sword and, being so close to the monster, would be burnt to a cinder by his fiery breath, or at least well scorched." "I believe you learned your own technique a little late," said Meghan to tease him; "did you not?" "Sir Henry's dragon," said Alisane loyally, "was almost fifty feet long, and poisonous to boot." "You did not tell me that," said Sir Henry, growing pale. "I did not want to worry you," said Alisane.

In such interesting ways our three travelers spent the week, while work progressed on Alisane's coach. However, life in the city was not altogether pleasant, for it was noisy at noon, and dangerous at night; the streets were dusty at times, and muddy at others, dirtying the ladies' gowns, no matter how daintily they stepped over the garbage and the dung. In hot weather, the smell was strong; and the townspeople were rude in every kind of weather.

And besides, Alisane was nursing a disappointment. For Sir Henry had said nothing more about marriage; there was a small cathedral in Chichester, but she could not get him into it. It seemed to her that each time they found themselves in that vicinity, Meghan discovered something to admire elsewhere. "There is an exhibition of juggling," she would say, "on the Common; let's walk over to watch it." Or: "Look: there is a knight on his way to the wars in the north; let us go talk to him." "I think you find much entertainment in the world," said Sir Henry. "Why so I do," she replied, "but even so, I would rather ride with you than anything I know of." "That is something to make a man feel marvelously proud," said Sir Henry.

Alisane was able to bring the cathedral to Sir Henry's attention only once. "It is not large," she said, "but sufficiently elegant; and with a handsome window in three colors. And the altar is lit with many tapers." "Why, splendid," said Sir Henry heartily. "That must make an agreeable illumination to God." "There is also a chapel," said Alisane, "for small occasions, such as weddings of no social importance." "Good," said Sir Henry; "that must be a great comfort to anyone wishing to be married." "Yes," said Alisane; "it must, mustn't it?"

And coming upon Manfred shortly afterwards in a passageway, she gave him a smart kick in the ribs. But she had no sooner done so than she sank to her knees beside him, and gathered him in her arms. "Forgive me," she said; and wept into his fur.

Manfred didn't mind; for he was enjoying life in Chichester; not being handicapped in any way by shyness or diffidence, he had already met a friend, with whom he had had several illuminating conversations. "To live in a great city," said the friend, whose name was Hoover, "has many advantages. One has as much company as one wants; and one is safe, or comparatively so, from the beasts of the forest and of the night." "There is something to be said for that," agreed Manfred, "for a cockatrice in moonlight is a horrid sight." "My goodness," said Hoover, "have you seen one?"

"Often," said Manfred. "What are they like?"
asked Hoover. "Ah," said Manfred; "what indeed?
I do not think I could describe it. Each time, to
see a cockatrice, is to die a little." "Well," said
Hoover, philosophically, "I would rather die a
little than all at once."

"Do you believe in the hereafter?" asked Manfred. "Yes and no," replied Hoover. "I think that
we are stewards of our lives, and will be punished
or rewarded for what we have done with them.
But what that property actually is over which we
exercise our stewardship, I do not pretend to
know." "My master thinks there is a heaven," said
Manfred, "to which, when he dies, he will be
transported in good state, and to the accompaniment of harp music." "With both ladies?" asked
Hoover in astonishment. "Certainly," said Manfred; "he would be in hell if he were obliged to
choose."

At the week's end, the coach was finished,
painted a serviceable green and lined in cherry-

colored silk as Alisane had wanted. It proved impossible for the carriage-maker to provide tassels of gold, but he made up for it by sewing a little fur muff for Alisane's feet, which he placed on the floor of the carriage, and which proved just the right size for her, and too small to accommodate Meghan's feet, which were larger. There was room, as the builder had said there would be, for all three travelers, and also their baggage; Sir Henry sat in front, along with his feather bed, his extra suit of armor, and his underwear, while the two ladies rode in back, upon a cushion. Sir Henry's spear was strapped to the roof of the carriage, while his sword and shield and helmet hung from Ponderer's saddle, clanking as they moved. The two horses, hitched to the whiffletree on either side of the wagon-tongue, stepped slowly and heavily along, drawing the carriage behind them; and so the entourage passed creakily out of town, and into the forests to the north.

CHAPTER

X

wherein Sir Henry meets a dispirited knight, and

Meghan meets with a disappointment

RAIN set in, sighing in the forest, dripping from the trees. The horses' hooves clumped dully on the wet leaves, and a small steam rose from their drenched flanks. But Sir Henry and the two ladies were warm and gay in their coach. "Now you see," said Alisane, "how right I was. And how wretched you would have been, seated on the slippery back of a damp horse, with the rain creeping down your collar, instead of leaning back dry and comfortable upon a silk cushion." "Yes, dear," said Sir Henry.

Meghan, tuning her lute, began to play a plaintive air.

"Wher hides the rose," she sang,
"Stole from a leydy's cheke?
Who knows?
Nay, do not seke
The Stolen budde, for fere thy queste
Lead thee too strait upon her breste."

"Charming," said Sir Henry; "charming. She has a sweet voice, has she not, Alisane?" "It is a sweet little voice," said Alisane, "but unschooled."

Toward noon they came into a kind of glade, where they found a drenched horse tethered to a tree, and a knight seated nearby, his visor closed and his sword in hand, but altogether mournful in appearance. Sir Henry stopped the horses, and reached apprehensively for his shield; but the knight made no move, and remained either asleep or sunk in dejection. "We need not disturb him," said Sir Henry; "we will go around the other way." "What," cried Meghan, "and miss an adventure?" "Well," said Sir Henry, "I do not know how this adventure might end." "Of course not," said Meghan, "so go and find out."

Sir Henry alighted from the coach, not at all willingly, and holding his sword at the ready, and covered by his shield, advanced toward the seated knight. "Whoever you are," he said, "stand up and declare yourself."

At this the strange knight sank even lower onto the wet grass, and opening his visor, fixed Sir Henry with a listless glance and replied:

"For what?"

"Why," said Sir Henry non-plussed, "for the usual reasons: for the usages of chivalry and the rules of knight-errantry."

The young man looked at him with contempt. Then he expressed himself in a simple buzzing sound, to which he added indifferently:

"Stop bothering me."

Very much surprised by this remark, Sir Henry also opened his visor, to get a better look at the stranger. He saw a young man, not at all bad-looking, but with a petulant mien, whose eyes were lackluster, and whose mouth drooped at the corners. "Do you mind if I sit down?" asked Sir Henry.

Letting himself down onto the grass, Sir Henry laid aside his shield, and stretched his legs out before him. "This is better," he said. "Perhaps you would not mind telling me your name?"

"Not at all," said the other. "It is Gosling."

"Well, then, Sir Gosling," said Sir Henry, "why do you dislike me, not knowing me?"

"There is nothing personal about it," said the knight; "I dislike everyone." "I would not think you old enough," said Sir Henry. "I am nineteen," said Gosling.

"Ah," said Sir Henry. "Then you belong to the younger generation."

Sir Gosling regarded him moodily. "I didn't ask to be born," he declared. "And I like nothing that I see in this world. I don't like sitting here in the rain, or talking to you; but if I stuck my sword in your ribs, I shouldn't enjoy that either, at least not for long enough to make it worth doing." And he added simply:

"I don't get a bang out of anything."

"That is truly pitiful," exclaimed Sir Henry, "when the world is so full of beauty and wonder."

Sir Gosling looked around him at the wet and dismal landscape, and allowed himself a sour smile. "In fifty years I'll be dead," he said, "and you even sooner. What's so beautiful about that? or something to wonder at?" And he added:

"It's got to go."

"You must have had a very unhappy life," said Sir Henry sympathetically; to which Sir Gosling replied simply:

"I have experienced everything."

"Dear me," said Sir Henry, "we must discuss this at greater lengths; but let us go back to the coach, where we can keep dry; and where my ladies are preparing a lunch." "I don't mind if I do," said Sir Gosling.

Back in the coach, the ladies Alisane and Meghan greeted Sir Gosling with friendly curiosity, and made room for him upon the cushion; Alisane urged him to remove his helmet, and Meghan placed a dish of meat pasty in his hands. Sir Henry then brought out a stoup of wine and a flagon of ale, and soon all four were relaxed and in good company with one another.

"It seems strange to me," said Alisane, "that one so young should be so bitter." "So would you be bitter, ma'am," said Sir Gosling, "if you were me. I have no liking for the world; or for what is in it." "Do you have no fondness for anything?" asked Meghan. "Well," said Sir Gosling thoughtfully, "I am very fond of ale."

"But surely," said Alisane, "being a knight, you do believe in chivalry?" "Why no," replied Sir Gosling; "it's all hard knocks, and endless journeys. That's all very well for old boys like Sir Henry here, who were brought up on it; but to me it looks like a fool's errand. Take Sir Lancelot."

"What about him?" asked Sir Henry. "He was a great knight," said Sir Gosling, "and a marvelous fighter, both in the French style and the English. But he was done in, irregardless. Lancelot is dead, from loving too much; and so are Guinevere and Arthur; and we have had our hearts broke in too many wars, and we are ruled by committees. It is in sorry state, this land; and I would rather not open my mouth in it." "Except to pour down the beer," said Alisane.

"Do you not believe in a better world?" asked Meghan. "I might," replied Sir Gosling, "if I could think of one. But no one has thought of one yet. The world is up to its neck in dung, and will be this next thousand years."

"And are all young people like you?" asked Alisane.

"Why not?" replied Sir Gosling. "They know that men are cruel and women untrue; that heaven is a dream, and pleasure is over too quickly. So do not talk to young men about a better world;

for there is none to be had." "If you think that women are untrue," said Alisane hotly, "you will end up by obliging them to be so."

And Meghan added:

"You have made no allowance for spiritual things."

"It seems to me," said Sir Henry ponderously, "that young people—if you do indeed speak for them—make a mistake in denying themselves that hope of the future, whether on earth or in heaven, which sustained my generation and the generations before me." "It did not keep you up very high," said Sir Gosling, "and you have been coming down ever since with a thin, sad sound like escaping air.

"If there is some ale left, I will have it," he concluded, holding out his goblet, "for although the laws of England and the rules of chivalry seem equally wormy to me, I am very fond of English ale."

Soon after this, the rain having let up, Sir

Gosling left them and returned to his horse, and the three travelers started out again in the fresh cold air and under the dripping trees.

"Do you know," said Meghan, "I am sorry for that young man; for I do believe he has not had a very happy life." "He has not had very much of any kind of life," said Sir Henry. "After all, at nineteen . . ." "I do not know why it is necessary for young people to be so rude," said Alisane.

A short while further on, Meghan begged them to stop, and excusing herself, climbed down from the coach. "I must have left my scarf behind me somewhere in the glade," she said, "and will just run back to see." "Why," exclaimed Alisane, "you were nowhere outside the coach the entire time; and your scarf is here, under your nose." "Well then," said Meghan, "it is something else, and I wish you would mind your own business." "We will go slowly on," said Sir Henry, "and you can catch up to us." "Yes, do," said Meghan, "and I will see you when I see you."

So saying, she ran lightly back through the woods over the way they had come, and was soon lost to sight.

Sir Henry and Lady Alisane proceeded on their journey, Sir Henry with the most uncomfortable thoughts, but the Lady Alisane in excellent spirits; and so made perhaps a mile, when looking back they saw the Lady Meghan running after them, her hair in disorder, and her skirt disarranged. Reining in the horses, Sir Henry halted the coach, and they awaited the damsel, who arrived out of breath, and in a state of discouragement.

"Some people," she said as she climbed back in, "don't understand a person's simple desire to be friendly."

The coach rolled on through the forest under the dark, wet trees, among which flitted from time to time the shy and shadowy deer. Sir Henry sat and gazed out of the window; he did not know what he thought, after all.

concerning the great battle in the forest

"I AM ashamed," said Ponderer, "to be seen hitched to this wretched wagon." "Why?" asked Simpkins placidly; "it is nice clean work; and as for your appearance, have you ever taken a good look at yourself when fully caparisoned for the joust, or armed cap-a-pie for battle? I assure you, you look like some immense worm." "I may look like a worm," said Ponderer, "but at least it is a large one. I do not look as though I were drawing a cart." "Well, somebody has to do it," said Simpkins philosophically.

While this conversation was taking place, Manfred had been ranging here and there in the forest, to the left and right of the road. And it was on one of these forays that he came upon a fresh and exciting scent, which first teased and then infuriated him, made his hackles rise and his hair bristle, and sent him, barking furiously, into the nearest thicket, from which, almost at once, he came bursting out again, in a startled manner, pursued by a wild boar.

This was in fact a more dangerous animal than a cockatrice, although Manfred did not know it; but instinct impelled him to run nonetheless, and run he did. And since instinct also drew him to the security of what passed for home and the advantage of his master, Manfred set out in a straight line for Sir Henry and the coach, yelping as he came.

"Hark," said Ponderer; "isn't that our friend, the hound? He sounds in trouble; and he is headed this way."

"Oh heavens," said Simpkins; "what now?"

At this moment Manfred burst from the forest, pursued by the savage boar, and circled the coach like a bee. The ladies screamed, the horses reared, and Sir Henry turned pale, and reached for his armor. "My love," exclaimed Alisane, "where are you going?" "This pig will kill both dog and horses too," replied Sir Henry from inside his helmet, "if I do not stop him."

So saying, he took his spear from the roof of the carriage, and making his way out over the dash-board, unhitched Ponderer from the coach, and got himself up onto his back. Freed of his responsibilities, Ponderer let out a contented whinny, and cantered off down the road.

"Whoa," cried Sir Henry, indignantly.

And turning his head, he tried to see what was happening behind him.

Manfred had by this time decided to go under the coach, which caused the boar to attack the vehicle itself; the ladies lay swooning with fright in each other's arms, and Simpkins stood trembling in the traces, with eyes closed, awaiting death. "Back we go!" cried Sir Henry, and pulling hard upon the reins, turned Ponderer about, and setting his one spur to his horse's flank, charged slowly down upon the boar, with spear in rest.

Manfred, meanwhile, had fled out from under the other side of the coach; and the boar, in following, had gotten itself beneath the wagon, and was ravaging about, which caused the ladies to scream louder than ever; for which reason Sir Henry, galloping in on the attack, found himself without a target, and was carried down the road a good fifty paces before he could check his career.

He then turned, to consider the situation, and to draw up his battle plans. "There is no doubt," he said to himself, "that this is a formidable adversary, being built so low, and therefore hard to hit with a spear; yet I must be very careful not to fall off my horse, for I would be at a disadvantage on the ground."

It was obvious that as long as the boar remained

under the wagon, he could not be reached, and that if he were left there much longer, he would end by destroying not only the coach, but the passengers as well. "Now by St. George," exclaimed Sir Henry, "was ever knight in a worse predicament?"

"Help!" cried Alisane. "Au secours!"

"I am coming," replied Sir Henry. "In a minute."

"It will be too late by then," said Alisane.

Meghan waved to him from the carriage window. "Don't just stand there," she shouted; "do something!"

And she beat with her heel on the floor of the coach. "Go away," she cried to the boar; "fight with Sir Henry, not us!"

Urged to approach a few steps closer to the coach, Ponderer did as he was told, but he was not at all eager for it. "It's all very well," he thought, "but if Sir Henry misses with his spear—and he is by no means what I would call an expert marksman—I could easily lose a leg. At least a leg," he added.

"Come out, accursed pig," called Sir Henry, "and face an adversary more worthy of you than a wooden coach and two frightened women."

The boar did not reply in so many words to this challenge, but backed slowly out from under the carriage, and turned to face Sir Henry. His little red eyes glared balefully at the knight, and with the sharp short scimitar of his tusk he made a few tight circles in the air, not unlike a fencer of the French School. Sir Henry kept the point of his spear carefully upon him, while Ponderer backed sensibly away; and Manfred gazed out at the scene from behind a tree.

"Come," said Sir Henry to his charger, "go forward, at a canter or at least a smart trot, because what you are doing is embarrassing me."

It was the boar, however, who moved first. After pawing the ground with his forefeet, and wriggling his behind, he bore down upon Ponderer and

Sir Henry, who kept his lance steadily upon him, though grown slightly pale; but Ponderer, seeing the fury of the animal's charge, first gave a jump sideways which caused Sir Henry to lose his stirrups and to cant or lean to starboard, and then a spring forward which carried him up past the charging boar and toward the coach, where Sir Henry did in fact fall off, and into the carriage on top of the ladies, who shrieked in terror at this unexpected turn of events, while Ponderer continued into the forest at a gallop.

"Pardon me," said Sir Henry, scrambling to his feet; and having lost his spear, looked about him for a weapon. But there was nothing handy except his stone hot-water-bottle. "Give it to me," he exclaimed; "I will throw it at him, like an arbalest." "Do not do so," cried Alisane, "for it will break, and you will have nothing for the winter." "If I do not stop this pig from attacking us," said Sir Henry, "I will not live to see the winter, or even the fall." "What about me?" asked Alisane indignantly. "Naturally, I included you," replied Sir Henry.

Meghan meanwhile had been watching the boar, and seeing that he was about to charge once more, this time directly at the carriage, asked leave of Sir Henry to put him off by means of the feather bed. "Much as they do in Spain," she said, "where they fight the bulls." "I'm afraid he will rip it to pieces," said Sir Henry, "and besides, you would be putting yourself in danger." "He may do the feather bed some harm," Meghan admitted, "but as you say, if we are not here this winter, we will not need it." "Well then," said Sir Henry, "do as you please, but do not take unnecessary risks."

Without losing any further time in discussion, Meghan seized the feather bed; and the boar at this moment being almost directly beneath the carriage window, she leaned perilously out, calling as loudly as she could:

"P-i-ig, Pi-i-g!"

The old boar glanced upward, raising his snout as he did so; and with a gasp Meghan flung the feather bed over him, like a net.

At once the boar exploded into the most violent action, rearing and ripping, bucking, snorting, tossing and twisting, and charging blindly, this way and that in an effort to dislodge the puff, which would not come off but scattered feathers like snow in all directions; and finally collided with one of Simpkins' hind legs, at which the trembling horse, who had been all but frozen with fear, felt such an access of terror that he lashed out with his hoof, and caught the pig squarely in the midriff, breaking several of his ribs, and knocking the breath out of him.

Seeing the boar breathless and motionless upon the ground, Sir Henry let go of Alisane, and hopping nimbly out of the coach, cut the boar's throat with his dagger. Meghan also descended from the carriage, and went to pick up what was left of the feather bed; but Alisane sat where she was, without moving. "I am glad to see how it is done in Spain," she said, "but I do not think it a proper sport for ladies."

Now that the danger was over, Manfred came out from behind his tree and Ponderer returned from the forest; but Sir Henry decided to remain where they were for the night, in order to get the greatest benefit from the pig, which he meant to serve for supper. A pit was dug, a fire built, and the pig laid upon it, and covered; and after pulling the coach off to one side of the road, where it would furnish them with a small but not uncomfortable night's lodging, our travelers relaxed, to rest and refresh themselves. The ladies found a clear stream nearby, in which to wash the dust from their cheeks, and Manfred stretched himself out near the barbecue pit, his nose upon his paw and pointed in the direction of the cooking.

Meanwhile, Ponderer, tethered with Simpkins to a tree, found himself faced with a puzzle. "Well, here we are," he said; "I, whose business it is to carry my master into battle, and you who do not believe in fighting; but which of us killed the boar? I ran away, and left you to deliver the mortal blow all by yourself." "It was a complete surprise to me," said Simpkins, "but I must admit, I was gratified by the speed and power of my reactions." "You are probably more powerful than you realize," said Ponderer, "and would be excellent in a massed charge." "Do you think so?" asked Simpkins in pleased tones. "I have always thought that it must be very difficult to be a hero, but perhaps it is not as difficult as it seems."

Night fell; and Sir Henry and the ladies, dining upon roast pork, were comfortable, and in pleasant spirits with one another. "I would not have believed," said Sir Henry, munching on a chop, and delicately licking his fingers, "that a maid and a feather bed could win such a victory." "Why," said Meghan modestly, "it was nothing; without you we should have been strewn all over the landscape." "There you go again," said Alisane, "mak-

ing a hero of him." "Why so he is," cried Meghan;
"and I wonder that you do not know it." "I know
that he would have broken his hot-water-bottle,"
said Alisane, "if I had not stopped him." "Would
you count a stone jug higher than a man's honor?"
asked Meghan. "His honor is loose on a horse,"
said Alisane, "as I have told him before." "That,"
said Meghan, "is a crude observation." "Oh well,"
replied Alisane sweetly, "I am not so spiritual as
you." "I am not so spiritual," said Meghan hotly,
"that I am eager to get to heaven before my time.
While you sat screaming, who was it killed the
boar?" "Simpkins," said Alisane.

"Ladies, please," said Sir Henry.

xïï

concerning natural man; and of Sir Henry's arrival

at Devizes

Now there passed several weeks in which nothing occurred to trouble or occupy them as they traveled through the forest already in its full dress of summer green; and the warm, aromatic days and cool sweet nights induced in Sir Henry and his companions a sense of well-being, of innocence, and joy. "For innocence," said Meghan, "is not a state physical, but a state spiritual, as is proved by the courtesan Thais, who turned out to be one of history's most innocent women after her conversion, while the monk Athanael, who converted her, ended up a prey to the most outrageous and guilty desires." "He could have offered to marry her," said Alisane, "and saved himself all that trouble."

Sir Henry was inclined to agree that there were advantages in marriage. "It is a fact," he said to Alisane, "that when I think of you, I am sweet and comfortable in spirit; I do not feel a desperate need to distinguish myself in the field, and have, instead, a tender impulse to stay at home, and to help with the housework."

"That is very dear of you," said Alisane. "But I cannot remember when you have ever done so." "There has never been any housework to speak of," said Sir Henry.

But the truth was, he could never quite make up his mind; for he no sooner found himself inclined one way than he began to lean the other. And though with Alisane, as he said, he saw himself at home, yet with Meghan he found himself dreaming of lands beyond the sea, and saw himself as in his youth, with his pennon flying in the wind and his armor bright again. "We will take my feather bed," he said, "and Alisane; and we will all ride out upon a quest together." "Why do we take Alisane," asked Meghan, "when she is such a home-body?" "I should be homesick without her," said Sir Henry simply.

"Well, then," said Meghan coolly, "stay at home; and I will take Simpkins, and find my own cockatrices." "I could not bear it at home," said Sir Henry, "if you were away."

Meghan was silent for a while considering; and then she sighed. "It must be hard to be a man," she said presently. "It is very lonely," said Sir Henry. And he added:

"The trouble is, I am not altogether a hero."

In time, the travelers found themselves in a strange part of the country, no longer in the green forest but among bare rocks and fields; and came one day in their coach to a hill, on which stood a knight leaning upon a great sword, and dressed all in silk of many colors, with no armor that they could see. And this knight was surrounded by others like him, and no maids or damsels were to be seen anywhere, but only several ladies in mannish attire, of a good age, and with their hair cropped close, like that of a page. However, the appearance of the ladies was outshone by the bright robes and ribbands of the men, who seemed to vie with each other in the fancifulness of their dress and appearance. "What have we here?" remarked Sir Henry, and stopped the coach, the better to observe this strange company.

The knight, who had been leaning on his sword, drew himself upright and addressed Sir Henry as follows:

"I am Sir Variant," he said, "who hold these lands in fief, fee, fee tail, and fee simple, along with all heroes, knights, poets, and troubadours, and none may stay here or perform here, either in feats of arms, or in verse plain or complain, or chant, or song romantic, or skill or art of any kind, unless he join my company."

"I do not think that I can join your company," said Sir Henry courteously, "for I have my ladies with me, and am besides in search of fame and fortune." "Why then," said Sir Variant heartily, "I can make you famous, for I control opinion in these parts, and in a large portion of the kingdom besides; and if you want a fortune, nothing is easier." "Even so," said Sir Henry obstinately, "I am minded to continue my quest, for I do not know what my ladies would find to do here." "Little enough," said Meghan, "if what I think is true; so let's away."

Sir Henry clucked to his horses, and gathering up his reins, inclined his head toward Sir Variant, and declared: "I thank you for your courtesy, Sir Knight; but I will take up my journey again to Tintagel by way of Devizes, where I hope to find some employment for myself, and amusement for

my ladies." "Since there are two of them," said
Sir Variant lightly, "they might learn to amuse
themselves together." "Why so we do," replied
Meghan pertly, "but not as you imagine, for we
fling plates and saucers at each other the livelong
day." "Well," said Sir Variant, "I suppose you
must do as you please; and if you will not give up
your journey, then you will not; but do not expect
me to sympathize with you, and as for fame, there
is no use your looking for it any longer." "And
why not?" asked Sir Henry in surprise. "Because,"
said Sir Variant, "in these lands, a man is counted
a member of the brotherhood, or he is not; and
no one with such a fondness for ladies can hope to
achieve renown, or remain anything but anonymous." "What brotherhood is that?" asked Alisane
innocently. "Why," said Meghan, "they are all
sticks in the same bundle."

Sir Henry continued on his way; and was surprised to observe the extent and wealth of Sir
Variant's lands. Wherever he looked, he saw castles

and keeps, of high style and ornament; yet the meadows surrounding them were bare, and the landscape forbidding. Here and there young boys were observed, flying their kites, or running and leaping together; but nowhere were maidens to be seen, playing on the grass. And since Sir Henry was not able to procure any food or drink in this country, either for himself or his ladies, they were in a pitiable state when they arrived at last under the green trees again, and were able to find a clear brook at which to quench their thirst, and some mushrooms and water-cress for their breakfast.

"It seems to me that we were in a great hurry to leave," said Alisane, "and that we might have been granted a castle, with many rooms and conveniences, if we had stayed." "Why so we might," said Sir Henry, "but we should have had to pay for it; and though I do long to become renowned, I prefer to do so in my own way, which is the way of most men, or at least it was when I was young."

Several days later they found themselves approaching Devizes, where King Anselm had his castle and held court, and here they found many other knights and ladies gathered for a Tournament of Love, and were made welcome at the castle, and given rooms in the east wing above the kitchens. After changing into clean kerchiefs for the ladies, and Sir Henry putting on a new silk doublet over his underwear, they went all three out into the warm summer sunshine to the meadow beyond the castle where the pavilions had been erected and the lists set up. The hucksters' booths were crowded with all kinds of trinkets and games of chance, a gallery and target for the longbow and crossbow, weights for lifting, an exhibition of dried butterflies, a contest of jams and pickles, and the showing of a two-headed calf; as well as a merry-go-round upon which Alisane and Meghan made several courses, Alisane seated upon a gryphon, and Meghan upon a unicorn. There, also, Sir Henry shot at a bladder with a longbow, but missed, and was coaxed to try his skill at decapitating a goose with his sword, but missed again, to Alisane's chagrin, for she was already in her mind basting the goose in one of the castle ovens. The Lady Meghan bought a ribband for her hair, and Alisane a faring; and both ladies had their palms read and their fortunes cast; Sir Henry treated them all to buns and honey and an ice and a pasty of prawns; and downed three flagons of ale, and then went back to behead the goose, but missed a second time. "I have never had such merriment," said Alisane.

In the evening, there was a mime, and a procession of illuminated floats representing the most famous Courts of Love, followed by a Parade of knights in all degrees of chivalry, complete with banners, marshals, heralds, pages, squires, knaves, trumpeters, grooms, and yeomen. There followed a charming rout of damsels, each dressed to resemble a flower, some being roses and others bluebells or dahlias, which made Alisane think of Alyot's castle, and caused her to become silent, and to give utterance to a sigh. "What is the matter, my dear?" asked Sir Henry considerately; "have you eaten too much?" "I was thinking of the illusion of beauty," said Alisane, "and that all must die and perish in the dust." "Lack-a-daisy," exclaimed Meghan, "what a time to turn liverish!" But Alisane did not take up the argument, for she was suddenly grown weary for some reason she could not account for. It seemed to her that here would be a proper place to be married, but that the time had already gone by for it to have meaning; and the church bells of Devizes, ringing like silver in the air, caused her only a gentle melancholy, and the thought that she was growing old, and that life had passed her by. "There was a cathedral at Chichester," she said, "with golden windows; it would have been lovely to remember, but we did not use it, and now I shall be twenty before long, and my youth is over, with all its sweet beauty, and I am practically an old maid." "You are talking nonsense," said Meghan; but she looked at her curiously, and was gentle with her for a while.

The evening ended with a great ball, in which Sir Henry danced first with Alisane, and then with Meghan, and then with both together, which caused some confusion in the turns, and in the do-si-do; after which the ladies danced with each other, and Sir Henry went in search of some ale to refresh his spirits.

While he was drinking his ale in the buttery, an elderly gentleman approached him, and after asking if he might stand with him, enquired courteously after his health, and whether he was comfortable. "Why," said Sir Henry, "I am very comfortable, thank you, and my health is good, all due to my excellent host, King Anselm, whom I have never met, and to his tournament, which I mean to avoid like the plague." The old gentleman expressed surprise at this, and asked Sir Henry if he did not intend to enter his name in the lists. "Many good knights have entered," he declared, "and there should be great honor and renown for the winner, in addition to the grand prize, and the opportunity to crown his lady." "I know," said Sir Henry with a groan, "but I must eschew it." "I did not take you for a feeble knight," said the old gentleman, "or a coward; but perhaps you are not adequately mounted, in which case there are horses to spare in the castle." "I am not at all feeble," replied Sir Henry, "and all too adequately mounted; for in addition to my own charger, I have another that has just killed a wild boar with a single kick. But even if you were the King himself, and did invite me by hand, I must decline, much as I would like the honor and renown, and that for a sound reason." "Well then," said the old gentleman, "I *am* the King, so let me hear your reasoning."

"Sire," said Sir Henry bowing low, "I have two ladies; and if I were to come out victor in the jousts, I must crown one of them Queen of Beauty."

"I see," said King Anselm.

"If you do," said Sir Henry, "you will understand my dilemma. For one of these ladies is my wife, though we have never been cathedral-wed, yet by precedence of seniority she does acquire title; and the other is no less my responsibility, I having won her from her lord in fair combat . . . or, at least, in combat of one sort or another . . . and one is the friend of my heart, and the other of my dreams, yet heart and dream are so intermixed and intermingled that I should bruise most mournfully the spirit of either one, were I to prefer the other. And to crown one Queen, and leave the other sitting uncrowned all in the public gaze would be an unknightly thing to do; nor could I crown a stranger, and so shame them both." "Of course," remarked King Anselm gently, "you have not yet been proven victor in even one preliminary bout." "That is true," said Sir Henry, "but think of the thumping I would have to give and take." "Heroes are often all over lumps," agreed Anselm. "Let us have another flagon of ale, because kings do not last forever, either.

"However," he said, "if you will not enter the tournament, promise me that you will stay for the banquet afterwards, when there will be some very interesting discourse on love, in which I would be glad to have you join." "I should be delighted to," said Sir Henry, "though I do not think I can add anything to the general knowledge of the subject." "No matter," said King Anselm, "for no one knows very much about it anyway."

xiii

of the Tournament of Beauty; and some lectures upon

an interesting subject

TRUE to his promise, Sir Henry remained at Devizes for the length of the tournament, and each day was more pleased with himself for staying out of it, as he watched the endless succession of knights charging down upon one another, and heard the crack of spear on shield or breastplate, and the rattling thump as the loser hit the ground. The Lady Alisane preferred not to attend the jousts, having a morning sickness, but the Lady Meghan took her place regularly in the pavilion, and did not miss a single day's tilt from the opening trumpet to the last. Without acquaintance among the competing knights, she nevertheless picked those she liked, and leaning prettily forward in her seat, her eyes shining and her lips parted, clapped her hands and cried encouragement and advice to her favorites. Her only disappointment lay in the fact that Sir Henry had not entered the lists; and she still hoped to prevail on him to do so, until Alisane pointed out to her certain renowned beauties among the damsels making up the Court of Love. "I see what you mean," said Meghan. "It is better for a knight not to be too famous, except posthumously." "There is enough competition between the two of us," said Alisane, "without calling in strangers."

"I have not meant to compete with you, Alisane," said Meghan, "though I have made no secret of my feelings; I did not choose my fate, any more than you did, and if my champion had slain Sir Henry, none of this would have happened." "We are like two cats," said Alisane, "with one piece of fish between us." "That is not a very nice way to speak of Sir Henry," said Meghan. "I will speak of my husband any way I like," said Alisane. "Why," cried Meghan, "he is not your husband, so far as I know."

"You are wrong," said Alisane, "for I feel already married to him, though without the consolations of the church." "I think the word is blessing," said Meghan. "That is what I meant," said Alisane. "And does that make you less fond?" asked Meghan. "No," said Alisane. "But I feel that I have a right to speak of him as I please, who have ever had his comfort and his good at heart."

"Well, then," said Meghan, "so you may; but I do not like to think of him as a piece of fish, for all I ever wished for him was only for his own honor and glory."

At the end of the tournament, and after the Queen of Beauty had been crowned, a banquet was held as advertised, at which Sir Henry found himself seated a little above the salt, but not so much as to be noticeable or embarrassing, while the Ladies Alisane and Meghan were invited to sit with the other gentlewomen in the gallery. A great repast was offered, consisting of a macedoine of fruit, an ox-tail soup, a stuffed carp, chicken with rice and peas, a salad of cold asparagus, a gooseberry fool, a trifle, and an ice. Then King Anselm rose, to welcome his guests, to thank all those who had competed in the lists, to offer homage to the Queen of Beauty, and honor to her champion, and to start the speeches.

"The Subject for tonight's discussion," he said, "is Love, of which we have all had some, or hope to have, and some perhaps too much, or some too little; but it is of all things the greatest mystery and cause of riot both in and out, for it has brought men up to heaven and down to hell, discovered wars, and set new dynasties upon their thrones. And this Subject, about which so much has been said and wrote, and so little known, has as many experts in its fields as there are men and women

In love; and it is from the most eminent of these that we have drawn our speakers for tonight, they being authorities on the Subject from our own court, so you may see Love both from its scientific and its poetical aspect; and we shall also hear from a distinguished guest, who is here upon his travels, and has had much practice in the practical aspects of this Subject; but I regret to say that I have forgotten his name." "Does he mean Henry?" asked Alisane. "I believe so," said Meghan. "Sir Variant said he would be anonymous."

"But first of all," said King Anselm, "I give you our own Sage and Doctor, Slesenger of Quibe, who has long advised us in matters scientific and political, and is also skilled in the treatment of humors, and the involvements of the heart. Dr. Quibe."

Slesenger of Quibe rose from his place next to the King, and after acknowledging the applause of the court, addressed the banquet as follows:

"Your Majesty, Ladies and Gentlemen: I am reminded of a story I heard the other day, about the elephant and the mouse. It seems that an elephant was marching through the jungle in a stately fashion, when looking down, he saw a small mouse cowering at his feet. Blowing a trumpet blast of disdain through his trunk, the elephant exclaimed: 'You worthless little creature, insignificant and inconsiderable, are you not ashamed to be so small and unrenowned?' To which the mouse, gazing up at the elephant from its meager perch upon the earth, replied sadly:

" 'I've been sick.'

"Well, gentlemen, he who loves is also sick; unless he has knowledge of love's meaning. For love, to most, is a kind of fever, or taking, with sleeplessness and difficulty of breathing, a state of flux, and a despondency of the blood. As in my retorts and alembics the gross metal when put to the flame sends up its bubbles and froth, having knowledge of gold in its secret depths, so desire rises in scum and nubilation through men's minds, having below it the true love. And to know love, man must first know himself, in depth, which is to say not in the mind, but in those secret places of the heart which are the child's first garden, where he plays among enchantments and spells whose power and danger he neither recognizes nor suspects."

"What has a mouse got to do with it?" whispered Alisane. "The mouse was sick," said Meghan.

Slesenger of Quibe continued:

"Who first touches a man's heart? His mother; or her opposite, which is to say, his nurse; or the kitchen maid; and for what else but one of these will he go searching through his life? Or, having one, will envy the other—or will seek both, all up and down the world. And so also a maiden her father, or his opposite, out of chagrin. But these they will often confuse, one with the other, and will not see them plain, and think that they have found paradise, and have found only some memory of childhood, or comforted some crying in the dark.

"So do not be too content in love, my lords and

ladies; for the truth is as hard to come by as the philosopher's stone and must be won by the same process of distillation.

"For you who wish to pursue this Subject further, I have tracts; or I will be in my office in the tower each morning from matins until noon."

After the Sage had seated himself, to the applause of the diners, the Court Jester, who was also of the order of troubadours, arose and addressed them as follows:

"Your Majesty; and you also there above me crowned Queen of Beauty, in whom we now delight; and maidens and damsels all, and noble lords: what is love but dreaming? For who has not waked from some sweet, troubling sleep, to find that what was ordinary has become overnight the world's very treasure, the familiar face touched suddenly with enchantment, the plain features turned lovely beyond anything, and all for no reason except that it was dreamed so? And who shall say whether it is real, or whether not? for beauty is only to the lover and beholder, and even a hawk in flight is not beautiful to a mouse." "There's the mouse again," whispered Alisane.

"And what is love but music, or moonlight and the smell of meadows? and what is that but dreaming? The world itself is little else but dream, half waking, half sleeping; and all the wisdom of the sages has not instructed us beyond this, or told us who sleeps. Therefore, my lords and ladies, be glad of beauty, and give it reverence; and do not ask the mind to feed the heart with the cold porridge of thought."

Taking his lute, the troubadour touched the strings, and sang to his own accompaniment the verses of Robert of Exeter:

But toe the lover, Beautye is hys love,
Hys herte's dere mystresse, ever at hys side;
Shee is the blue bright winde of hevven above,
The light of evening on the valleys wide.
Shee is the sea, shee is the swifter tyde

Of narrower waters, and the foreste greene;
In all hys courses, Beautye is hys guide,
She goes before him, shee is heard and seene,
And has a bodye. Lette the lover tell
Whose voice hee heares in music's swetest
*   parte;*
He knowes the face of Beautye, knowes it
*   well,*
Shee is hys friend, the Treasure of hys hearte,
Which on the Earth like benediction poures
A light hee loves, a Sperit hee adores.

The troubadour had no sooner seated himself, to
the sound of a gentle sighing from the ladies' gallery, than Sir Anyst of Aminweigh, the winner of
the tournament, rose in his seat to have his say. He
was a broad and burly man, well bruised, and
held together by bandages, and wearing the scars
of many combats and jousts.

"There is nothing better in the world," he said,
"than fighting and loving; and a man should not

choose one over the other. For this is the way of great fighters, to love the thing they kill; and this is the way of love, to take death, and make friends with it. For the moment of truth is both death and love. I have had many young men follow me, but they do not know this, and they do not have greatness. I am not young any longer, but I have crowned my lady Queen of Beauty because she is a fine golden girl, and love is not running away from what is brave and beautiful."

When Sir Anyst was finished, he sat down; and the Queen of Beauty threw him a kiss from the gallery. Then the King arose to introduce Sir Henry.

"Of our next speaker," he declared, "I shall say little; except to remark that he is a stranger to us, and that I have just remembered his name; it is Sir Clarence of Brentwood, son of Sir Beverly of The Glen."

So saying, he bowed graciously to Sir Henry, who rose diffidently to his feet. "He is not even anonymous any more," whispered Alisane. "Poor

Henry." "Hush," said Meghan; "it will be interesting to hear what he has to say."

"Your Majesty," said Sir Henry; "Noble Lords,
Knights, Ladies and Gentlemen:

"After the great speeches I have heard here this
evening, I am somewhat loath to follow, for though
I can tell you about a great many things—such as
the preparation of swivets for a stew, and the practice in Spain, where ladies do battle with bulls,
armed only with a feather bed—I have but little
knowledge of the subject of tonight's discussion. I
can tell you something about dragons and sorcerers; but about love, I cannot tell you anything at
all."

"I am not surprised," said Alisane. "No," said
Meghan, "but I am disappointed."

"For I think," said Sir Henry slowly, "that love is
a searching, and a quest, for something far away;
and is, like fame and fortune, to be found only
along the northern marches, or in the south ridings.
Or perhaps it is still more distant, in those western

lands beyond the sea, where the great monsters are; or it is expected tomorrow, or remembered from yesterday. And so there must ever be a sadness about it, such as one feels on hearing music distantly, or of an evening in the spring, with its sweetness and its sorrow. And that is all I have learned about it, my lords and ladies, in my travels; that it is a distant singing, and a sound of peace."

So saying, he sat down, amidst silence. Sir Anyst peered gloomily into his cup; and the troubadour drummed with his fingers on the table. But Meghan sat biting her nails, with a bleak look on her face; and Alisane wept.

xiv

in which Manfred experiences a grief

WHILE all this was going on, Manfred was not exactly idle, and managed to enjoy not only the high-
lights of the tournament, but the remains of the
banquet, in company with a poodle named Lettice. Brought up as she was in a castle, and used to
the protocol of the court, she found herself attracted despite herself to Manfred's rough exterior
and rude forest ways, and listened to his stories,
not all of which were true, with shining eyes and
an expression of interest and respect.

"I went through the wagon," he said to her, "and
underneath it and out the other side; and ma-

neuvered the boar; and I felt fine. The boar charged, and my friend put one hoof into his ribs. It was clean, and beautiful." "I wish I had been there," said Lettice.

"What I like," said Manfred, "is that moment of truth, when it's either you or the boar." "You sound like Sir Anyst," said Lettice. "Only in a small way, I'm afraid," said Manfred, "but it is a great compliment.

"Do you enjoy this life?" he asked later, watching Lettice crack a bone in her teeth. "To me, it has such a quality of over-stuffed comfort." "What else is there in the world but comfort?" asked Lettice. "Why," cried Manfred, "there is hunting and fighting, and the wet woods in the morning, and the sweet-smelling meadows at noon, with rabbits popping up all over like toadstools."

"I go out to the meadows sometimes," said Lettice, "with my master and mistress; but they are usually hawking, and I am not allowed to chase anything. I wish I had wings, and could stoop at a rabbit." "If you had wings," said Manfred, "you would be an angel."

"There are no poodles in heaven," said Lettice sadly, to which Manfred replied boldly: "I will put some there."

"But do you really like me?" she asked after a while. "It is so easy to be mistaken. I suppose I have not learned the really important things. I can walk on my hind legs, and jump through a hoop, and roll over; but I would starve in the woods, all by myself." "I wouldn't worry if I were you," said Manfred; "you will never be all by yourself." "How charming of you to say that," declared Lettice. "But one grows older and one meets so few really sympathetic souls—whom one could call a friend. . . ."

At the same time, she came close to him, and shyly touched his ear with her cold, delicious nose. "I like you, Manfred," she declared. "I think we could be friends. . . ."

"I have never been so happy," said Manfred.

"Have you really slain a gryphon?" asked Lettice, opening her eyes very wide, and at the same time giving him a tender look. "Several," said Manfred. "I never knew a real hero before," said Lettice; "it makes me feel very small and humble." "It is nothing," said Manfred. "Think nothing of it."

That night Manfred said to his friends Ponderer and Simpkins:

"I am thinking seriously of giving up this life of wandering, and establishing myself at court."

"As what?" asked Ponderer. "Something under a wagon?" "That is not very kind," said Manfred. And Simpkins also indicated surprise at his friend's remark.

"After all," he declared, "I can see where someone might find life at court more sympathetic than in the field, though I myself am eager for fresh battles and adventures." "Well, well," said Ponderer; "one victory, and he is off to the wars."

"It is not," said Manfred stoutly, "merely a matter of comfort; because I find that I am interested in culture and refinement." "You could scarcely have found this out by yourself," said Ponderer; "I wouldn't be at all surprised if some female were not mixed up in it." "Well," said Manfred modestly, "you know how it is." "Only by hearsay," replied the horse.

Manfred joyously told his friends about Lettice. "She has been gently reared," he explained, "but she enjoys coursing and would like to stoop at a pigeon. We have a great deal to offer each other." "That is as it may be," said Ponderer, "but you must admit that you are offering her little more than the chance to catch cockleburs in her coat. As for you, I can see you lying under the table, with greasy paws, and fat as an innkeeper; but how long do you think it would last? She is attracted to the bohemian in you, my friend—to the wanderer and hunter." "Do you always have to have me underneath something?" asked Manfred.

"Leave the poor fellow alone," said Simpkins gently; "he is a sad dog, or will be." "I don't know what makes you think so," said Manfred; and went off to find Lettice in the kitchen.

But Simpkins was right; for when it came time for our travelers to leave Devizes, Manfred was given his demission, and told, in a sweet way, but firmly, to go along with them. "It's been fun," said Lettice, "but all good things must end; and so must this. You are very attractive; and in many ways I wish it could go on. But we cannot escape our natures, and must face the facts: which are that our natures are not at all alike. We come from different backgrounds, and have not had the same opportunities; and the truth is, our tastes are not really the same. I have a softness for music and poetry; and at bottom you are a fighter." "Good heavens," exclaimed Manfred, "what gave you such an idea?" "Did you not maneuver the boar?" replied Lettice. "And several gryphon?"

"Well, then," said Manfred sadly, "goodbye; but I shall remember you all my life." "Yes, do," said Lettice sweetly, "and I will do the same for you."

Our travelers now set out upon the road once more, with gifts from King Anselm: a smoked ham, a cheese, two live ducks, silk handkerchiefs for the ladies, and an amulet for Sir Henry, carved from the horn of a unicorn; and seated together in their coach, the ladies reviewed the events of the past week. "It is too bad that no one asked me for my opinion of love," said Alisane, "because I would have told them." "Told them what?" asked Sir Henry comfortably. "That it is a state," said Alisane simply, "to which a woman gives herself wholly, and receives in return a baby and some instruction in cooking."

"My dear," said Sir Henry, very much moved, "I did not know." "Well, you know now," said Alisane, "and I think you had better find us a dry roof somewhere, before the winter storms set in." "I shall look for one at once," said Sir Henry.

And he added, a little doubtfully:

"Should we not be married, then?"

"That is a kind offer," said Alisane. "But it does

not come from your heart." "Well," said Sir Henry, "it may not, but it comes from somewhere very close." But Alisane only smiled sadly, and shook her head. "It is not near close enough," she said, "as I did discover at Devizes."

Trotting along a little in advance of the coach, Manfred remarked to his friends, Ponderer and Simpkins:

"I can tell you what love is. It is a hole inside the heart, into which has been emptied all the sadness of life. And this is something you carry around with you, day in and day out; and wake up with in the morning, and take to bed with you at night." To which Ponderer replied: "It is much better to have something to be sad about than never to have had anything at all."

Shortly after this Manfred surprised a small stoat in a thicket, and by boldness and good fortune caught the little animal by the neck. The dying stoat turned a look of great sadness and reproach on the hound, who held him in his jaws, and looked down his nose at him. "Why do you kill me," he asked, "when I have not done anything to you?" To which Manfred replied:

"It is a harsh world, my friend."

"Well," said the stoat before he expired, "I do not see that you are doing anything to make it less so."

in which Sir Henry is met with silence

SIR HENRY turned west from Devizes, and south, and headed toward Tintagel. He felt his responsibilities; and looked everywhere for a small castle or keep, not too strongly defended, which he could win for himself and family, either by force of arms or in exchange for his coach; but nothing appeared available. He passed several fine seigniories, whose owners, standing comfortably upon their battlements, either disdained to reply to his challenge, or angrily told him to move on. "This is a shocking state of affairs," said Sir Henry; "I am discouraged at the housing situation in this part of the country." "Perhaps we should seek a warm spot on the Cornish coast," said Meghan, "and winter in our wagon." "That might be all right for you," said Alisane. "But I shall need more room."

One day, a little more than a fortnight after leaving the court of King Anselm, Sir Henry found himself, at sundown, approaching a large and solid farmhouse. No smoke rose from the hole in the roof, which served as chimney; and no odor of cooking was in the air; but to one side of the road stood a large and menacing figure, dressed in rusty armor, and with his visor down. Unhitching Ponderer from the wagon, Sir Henry climbed upon his charger, and approached this guardian, who stood between him and the westering sun, and halted a short distance away. "I take it," he said, "that you are warden of this keep, or seigniory, or possibly farm, and might be willing to dispute its ownership with me."

As the figure made no reply to this statement, apparently disdaining either to affirm it or deny it, Sir Henry continued:

"I must find quarters for my ladies, and in particular for the Lady Alisane, and I will do combat with you if you wish, or perhaps you would like to travel and see the world in a truly novel and comfortable way, in which case I will exchange your keep for my coach, in which you will find every modern convenience."

However, the guardian said nothing, but continued to turn on Sir Henry his unwavering regard. Sir Henry sighed, and backed Ponderer a little further away. "I do not understand men's manners hereabouts," he said; "one would almost think that ownership of real estate was restricted in this vicinity."

He continued:

"My name is Henry of Brentwood; and I charge you, whoever you are, to defend yourself and your house, agreeing that if you overthrow me in fair combat you will come into my property, consisting of two horses, a coach, two damsels, one suit of armor, a hot-water-bottle, and a feather bed in need of repair.

"Will you defend?"

The breeze of evening stirred in the trees; and against the light it seemed to Sir Henry that the strange knight nodded his head ever so slightly. "Very well," said Sir Henry; "will you mount? or shall we fight upon the ground?"

Receiving no answer, Sir Henry found himself growing irritated. "What is holding you up?" asked Meghan. "This cursed fellow won't talk to me," replied Sir Henry. "He won't agree upon the rules." "Then make them up as you go along," said Meghan.

"Very well," said Sir Henry. And addressing both damsels in a grave voice, he bade them farewell. "My dears," he said, "it is quite possible that I may fall, a victim of this dour householder and to my desire to provide you both with a home. Remember me; and teach our children to be proper men and women, depending upon their sex." "I did not expect to have so many," said Alisane.

Sir Henry then laid lance in rest, and clapping his single spur to Ponderer's side, and with the cry "Esperans!" bore down upon the helmeted figure, who awaited his charge with imperturbable calm.

It was not surprising for Sir Henry to miss his first course altogether; and so he did on this occasion also, galloping past his adversary, who did not even bother to duck. Sir Henry pulled Ponderer up, and wheeled, and cantered back again, only to find the knight's back turned contemptuously toward him.

Sir Henry halted his charger and strove for a good two minutes to master his irritation. He thought of the rules of chivalry, he tried to remember his vows as a knight, and he counted to ten; but it was all in vain. "Very well," he said at last;

"if you will not turn around, you will not; and since you have no manners, I shall run you down from the rear as well as from the front, and with equal satisfaction."

So saying, he clapped spur once more to Ponderer, who sprang nimbly forward; and Sir Henry's lance, truly aimed for once, rang squarely upon the householder's back pauldron, lifting him into the air, and toppling him over; at which his armor came apart, and strewed the field with his insides, which turned out to be merely bundles of straw. "Good heavens," exclaimed Meghan, "we have conquered a scarecrow set to frighten away the birds." "I am glad he did not beat Sir Henry, then," said Alisane, "for it would have made me sneeze horribly."

Sir Henry did not allow his ladies' laughter to embarrass him for very long, but went off in search of the owner of the farmhouse. Presently he came back again, with a long face. "There is no one here," he said. "The place is deserted." "All the better," said Alisane; "then we won't have to fight for it."

This did not satisfy Sir Henry at all. "Possession by might," he declared, "which is to say by force of arms, or force majeur, is clearly defined, and relatively simple; the old owner is dispossessed by the new owner, and there you are. But possession by law is something else again, and brings you into contact with the legal mind, than which nothing is more appalling. There is the matter of claim, stake, right, and title; easement, right of common, right of user, fief, fee, fee tail, and fee simple, estate in fee, estate tail or in tail, estate in tail mail; alodium, free-hold; copyhold, leasehold, remainder, and estate in expectancy; to say nothing of escrow, which is a way of keeping everybody on tenterhooks." "I am going to look at the kitchen," said Alisane, "and see if there is room in it for my pots and pans."

The farmhouse proved to be commodious, and reasonably dry; and Alisane and Meghan cheerfully set about moving in, without worrying about who owned it. Sir Henry sought out the stables, and bedded down his horses, and found a shed in which to store the coach out of the weather. He found some salad greens growing in a small patch near the midden; also some roses, and several clumps of herbs, which he knew would please the Lady Alisane. An archery butt behind the house suggested that the owner had practiced upon the long bow, which worried Sir Henry for a while; but coming upon a modest graveyard, with several freshly cut inscriptions, he decided that the owner and his family must have perished either in the wars or of the plague, and had been buried, and would not be likely to bother him.

The house, of wood and stone, was of solid construction, and Sir Henry thought that it needed only a moat dug around it and a small tower, to serve as a modest keep. There was room near the stables for a tiltyard of sorts; and a supply of firewood had been piled near the chimney. "It is certainly not Joyeuse Garde," said Sir Henry, "or even Alyot's castle in the Wastes of Ende; but it will do for a while until I can find something better." At the same time, he remembered that Arthur himself had started modestly, "although he was," he admitted, "younger to begin with."

That night, as they sat in front of the bright fire in the kitchen, with its dark wood reflecting the rosy flames, dipping their bread into the bowls of rich broth which Alisane had prepared from the boar's thighbone, a cabbage, some dried peas, sorrel, and sage, they all agreed that they had never been more comfortable, not even at Devizes.

"I can tell you," said Sir Henry, "when my spear caught that fellow on the pauldron and lifted him into the air, it was quite a shock to me. Now, as I think back on it, I am sorry he turned out to be a haystack and not a man of flesh and blood, because I do not often run such a true course or handle my spear so expertly. But when one needs it, one doesn't have it."

"Well," said Alisane, "I am glad it turned out the way it did, for I should have hated to have had you overcome by a scarecrow." "Many men have been frightened by scarecrows," said Meghan, "and some have died of it." "He didn't frighten me," said Sir Henry; "I pitchforked him royally.

"Tomorrow," he added, "I shall look about a bit; for I have an idea that we shall find some cattle and sheep in the meadows belonging to the farm, and possibly some chickens that may have wandered away." "Oh," said Alisane, "it would be famous to have our own milk and cheese, eggs, butter, and pasties; to say nothing of wool for carding."

"For myself," said Meghan, "I intend to saddle Simpkins, and ride out into the forest, to see who our neighbors are." "Do you think we have neighbors?" asked Sir Henry. "I should be surprised if we had none," said Meghan. "Well," said Sir Henry doubtfully, "just so long as they are agreeable."

"If I do not come back in two days' time," said Meghan, "it will be because they are ogres. Or else," she added airily, "they will have proved agreeable beyond anything." "Perhaps I had better go with you," said Sir Henry, "for protection." "You had better stay right where you are," said Alisane, "because if anyone is going to be protected, it is me." "Yet Meghan is riding out alone into the forest," said Sir Henry. "Do not worry," said Alisane; "it is for her spirit's sake."

xvi

wherein Sir Henry builds his house

THE days passed; and the weeks passed; and Sir Henry busied himself with his estate. It took a good deal of work, to turn the farm into a castle, even a small one; and although Meghan helped as much as she could, Sir Henry had to do most of it himself. He dug the moat, while Meghan kept the ground moist for him; he hitched a scoot, or drag, to the horses, and brought stones in from the fields to build his tower; and set them one on top of another while Meghan held the plumbline, and kept the plaster wet. Together, on Ponderer and Simpkins, they rounded up a dozen cows, and a few sheep, and penned them for the winter; Sir Henry took his two-handed sword out into the pasture and cut hay with it, which Meghan bound with flax, for storing.

The summer waned, and autumn set in; and Alisane put up preserves and jellies. The nights grew cold; the rains came sighing across the meadows, and the fallen leaves, sodden with the drenching, gathered in ragged heaps on the ground. There was the good smell of wood fires and leaf smoke in the air, of grapes, and cider from Sir Henry's apple-press; and mornings, as the mists rose, the cattle stood with foggy breath and frosty flanks in the early light.

In the house all was comfortable and well arranged, except for Meghan's room, which was usually in a state of cheerful disorder. But strangely enough, Alisane didn't seem to mind, or perhaps even to notice it. For Alisane was unusually gentle these days, and quietly busy with her household tasks, and content; she even sang a little to herself,

some songs of her childhood, and swept and pol-
ished and cooked, and fed the hens and milked the
cows and carried water without complaint. Sir
Henry helped her often, when he could; but she
didn't ask him to, or seem to mind when he was
busy elsewhere. "It's my own home, Harry," she
said, "and I love it. I'm getting it ready for Abigail." "Abigail?" said Sir Henry; "I had hoped it
might be Gareth." "Abigail," said Alisane.

She did, however, take Sir Henry's hot-water-
bottle, and his feather bed, both of which he was
glad to lend her for the winter, preferring himself
to sleep before the fire, wrapped in his cloak.

In their stalls, the horses were becoming fat;
and Manfred was growing lazy. The days and
nights grew colder; there was rime on the meadows, and ice at morning in the ponds; and light
snows fell. It was comfortable for the old hound
indoors, before the fire—though somewhat smoky;
there was little pleasure to be found sniffing in the
frosty thickets, or running up and down over the

hard ground from which the best smells had disappeared. He thought of Lettice; already she seemed far away, a distant memory, part of a dream.

As the winter wore on, neighbors came to call at the farm; they brought gifts, suckling pigs, haunches of venison, small barrels of ale. Sir Henry entertained them with tales of adventure, out of his past; while Meghan sang ballads, accompanying herself on the lute. Alisane, in her gentle way, made everyone feel at home, and spent long hours in the kitchen, baking cakes and tarts for the company; there were square dances, rounds, catches, and games of forfeit, from which Alisane excused herself because of her condition. And when the cold winter moon rose over the snowy fields, Meghan before the fire in the firelight told the story of Arthur and Merlin, while the company roasted chestnuts in the flames, and drank mulled wine.

Among the gifts brought to Sir Henry that winter was a hooded tercel, or male goshawk, complete with glove, leash, hood, and jesses; and Sir Henry had flown him first on creance, and later free from the fist, and had found him in yarak, which is to say good order, and not inclined to bate. The falcon's perch being set near where Manfred liked to lie, the two became friends, were courteous to each other, exchanged opinions from time to time, and discussed the weather.

"Winter is a time of death," said the tercel. "There are few small birds or animals about; the fields are empty, everything sleeps. Yet for a hawk it has its advantages, because against that snowy silence the slightest sound or movement is instantly noticed; and when the thickets are bare it is much easier to stoop at whatever is under them. Therefore I enjoy this empty season; you might say I benefit from the depression." "So do I," said Manfred lazily, "because I do not have to go outdoors at all." "Not at all?" asked the falcon. "Only in the morning," said Manfred, "and again at night."

"We are different that way," said the hawk.

He continued: "I love to walk upon the wind, to slide down the currents of the sky, to mount in spirals, leaning on the air. But it has always vexed me not to be able to walk on the earth also. Even a mouse can walk better than I. A duck can swim; so could my ancestors. All I can do is fly." "It is an age of specialists," said Manfred.

"And for that reason," he went on, "I prefer to rest here, among my memories. I too have been a specialist in my field, both in loving and fighting. I fought the boar, I killed the stoat, and at court I excelled in even more gallant affairs. When I remember those moments in my life, I am happy." "You probably add a little to them here and there as you go along," said the hawk. "Why not?" asked Manfred. "If one sets out to make oneself happy, there is no use being stingy about it."

"Mine is a lonely life," said the hawk, "and my relations with other living creatures are usually of short duration, and over very soon. Nobody likes me, but everybody knows that I am there; and this means a great deal to me." "You could always learn to sing," said Manfred, "and get the same results."

Toward the end of February, a great stag was seen in the forest; and news of a meeting being brought to the house, Sir Henry saddled Ponderer, called his hound, and taking the tercel on his fist, set off to join the hunt. But he had not gone a mile in the woods before Meghan came galloping after him on Simpkins. "Wait for me," she cried, "for it will be a famous go, and I do not want to miss any of it." "Well then, come along," said Sir Henry resignedly, "but be sure not to turn out at the fences." "What a filthy idea," said Meghan. "I never refused a fence in my life."

The gentry met at Chumley Farm, some half-dozen knights, and as many squires and farmers, armed with crossbows, spears, and short hunting swords. Meghan was the only lady present, but sat her horse with such an easy air that everyone admired her. The dogs, including Manfred, were gathered, and then loosed, and the hunt moved

[163]

slowly through the forest, following the hounds who ran about, treeing chipmunks, startling mice, and chasing rabbits. "I wish we might get out of the trees," said Meghan, "for I should like a good gallop, with the wind in my face." "The wind is still a little cold," said Sir Henry, "for that sort of thing."

At Braxton Water the hounds picked up the stag's scent, and then away they went in good earnest, the hunters following in order of precedence, the knights first, and the yeomen after. Meghan was allowed to lead the way, out of deference to her sex, while a huntsman with his horn brought up the rear. It was in fact a cheerful sight, the bright pennants flying, the knights in their blue and crimson cloaks, with breastplates, greaves, and morions all shining in the sun, the yeomen in their buff and yellow jerkins, and all the sweet colors sharp and bright against the snowy ground.

The stag broke from the woods at Mooreton Meadow, and the hunt followed after, streaming out across the rolling fields, with Meghan still ahead and taking her fences lightly as thistledown. The huntsman blew his horn; and Sir Henry, encumbered with his spear in one hand, and his hawk on the other, rose with Ponderer to a low stone wall, and came down alone, without his horse and without his hawk, in a clatter of armor; and lay there, flat on his back with the wind knocked out of him. The hunt, with Meghan sailing on ahead, the horn playing bravely and Manfred panting along in the rear, went on up a rise and over a hill and into the woods again; and the stag, doubling back, came charging down across the meadow, and headed for the low stone wall.

The stag saw the outstretched figure of Sir Henry all too late. He was already gathered for the jump, and going fast; he tried to check his leap, to swerve in mid-air—even, for one desperate moment, to go backwards; but instead, caught his left hind leg in a stone, toppled, crashed within a yard of Sir Henry, and broke his neck.

"What I always say," said Alisane that night, when Sir Henry came home with the antlers, the tail, and most of the venison, "is you're either lucky, or you're not."

Three weeks later, with only Meghan to help her, the Lady Alisane was delivered of a bouncing girl. And as Meghan held her gently in her arms after her labor, Alisane smiled up at her weakly. "I have called you many names," she said, "and not all of them friendly. But in the end, it was you who held me, and went with me as far as you could, through the dark valley. What shall I call you now, sister and friend?"

Meghan bent down to kiss Alisane's wet, cold cheek. "Call me Aunt Meghan," she said.

concerning Sir Henry's last quest

SPRING came back to the meadows, the pussy-wil-
lows showed their little mouse-like buds, violets
were found in the woods. The trees put out their
haze of leaves; mists lay in the hollows at night,
and the peepers sang in the grass. Evening was a
long time, the rose died slowly in the west, there
was gentleness in the air, and longing in the heart.

And Meghan and Sir Henry walked in the garden, beside the moat, where as yet there were no
swans, though a family of ducks paddled among
the weeds in the shallow water. "Every day now,"
Sir Henry said, "new birds come to nest and sing

in my trees. And I have been thinking of the old stories of knights and heroes, and of the lands beyond the western sea." "It is questing weather, for sure," said Meghan. "I know," said Sir Henry. "I thought you would think so."

He fell silent for a moment; and sighed. "I am not thinking of a very long quest," he said; "only a very small one; and then home again. Just to see what lies over the hill." "I know," said Meghan. "I knew that you would understand," said Sir Henry; "dear Meghan."

"I doubt if Alisane will like it," he added doubtfully.

"She may not care," said Meghan, "being so taken up with Abigail."

Sir Henry nodded his head thoughtfully. "That's true," he said; "I had forgotten. A darling child, and a true Brentwood. I shall be glad not to hear her for a while in the early morning. Still, I should hate to hurt Alisane's feelings. . . . She might re-sent my leaving her, just at this time." "I scarcely think so," said Meghan.

But Sir Henry was not convinced. "She would miss me, I think," he said; and sounded a little obstinate about it. "Of course," said Meghan; "of course she would. We all will."

Sir Henry stopped walking, and stared at her. "What do you mean?" he asked. "What is that—'we all will'?" "Why," said Meghan, "I mean that go you must, as I well know, for you were born to errantry, and the spring is in you. And so we'll all miss you, all three of us." "You mean to say you are not going with me?" cried Sir Henry. "Not this time, my dear," said Meghan.

Sir Henry was thunderstruck. "But it was always you," he said, "who spoke the bravest." "Perhaps I did," said Meghan, "but it was you who did the deeds." "I did some for your sake," said Sir Henry, "and some for Alisane's; but it seems to me that I was always unhorsed."

Meghan's eyes were gentle when she answered him. "You did your best," she said; "and so you always will; and what more can anyone? But a woman's happiness is in her home; and Alisane has such happiness that it spills over a little, onto me." "And the Grail?" asked Sir Henry, "which was the utmost quest?" "I am no longer in such a fret to find it," she replied, "since I have held in my hand the little silver cup from which Abigail spoons her porridge."

She continued: "Wherever you go, you know that my thoughts will follow you. You are my dear knight; and my thoughts will be your attendants, your page and your squire. My proud thoughts, and my gentlest; my hopes and my dreams. If I had ambitions, Henry, they were for you, not for me. It is your fame which sheds its sweetness upon me, and fills me with a feeling of delight."

"Then was it just for me," asked Sir Henry, "or for my sake, that you sought for glory?" "For whom else?" replied Meghan simply. "I thought to help you to it." "I see," said Sir Henry. And he added quietly: "I'm afraid I shall find it very lonely."

Sir Henry made his preparations slowly; for although he was determined to go off on a quest of some kind, even a small one, a weekend or overnight, a good deal of the pleasure seemed to have gone out of it. And Alisane did not help very much, by acting about as Meghan had expected, and not appearing to care one way or the other. Alisane's figure had filled out, her expression had gentled, and she hummed to herself as she bent over Abigail in her crib, or bubbled her on her shoulder. There was a tranquillity about Alisane that Sir Henry found very irritating.

He made a point of sharpening his weapons and shining his armor in front of the fire at night, and talking loudly to Manfred as he did so. "Well, old boy," he would exclaim, "we'll be off soon, to new adventures, to fresh dragons and interesting sorcerers. And who knows what we'll come up with? Just to be out in the sweet woods again in the early morning; and to fall asleep when the sickle moon is in the treetops, under the starry sky." "The night air is not good for children," said Alisane.

"There is a bad hole in my doublet," said Sir Henry; and glanced hopefully at Alisane out of the corner of his eye. But Alisane and Meghan had their heads bent together, measuring out squares of linen for Abigail. "I will make her a little jacket of rabbits' fur," said Alisane, "for the winter." "I would rather find some ermine for you," said Meghan; "it is richer than rabbit."

"Never mind, Manfred," said Sir Henry; "we will get a new doublet as a prize somewhere."

Manfred wagged his tail doubtfully, and gazed up at his master with a certain uneasiness. He didn't know what Sir Henry was saying; but the sight of all those preparations aroused his gravest fears. The spring was not in him, except in somnolence; the last thing in the world he wanted to do was to leave his comfort, and go in search of cock-atrices.

"Of course," said Sir Henry mournfully, "we may never come home again; and our bones may rot and bleach among the stones of some unknown meadow." "For the summer rash, or itch," said Meghan to Alisane, "there is a marvelous powder made of chalk ground very fine; the country herea-bouts is full of it." "I know," said Alisane. "It is also very good when mixed with lavender."

"I have not even got a tercel," said Sir Henry.

As the days went by, his preparations proceeded more and more slowly. There was so much to do— or so it seemed; pots and pans to be brought to-gether for the journey, food to be provided, ale to be sought, his feather bed to be aired and well shaken out, his stone hot-water-bottle to have a new cover, his sword to be sharpened. Then Pon-derer must be shod, and his harness treated with vegetable fat and lye, his winter coat well brushed out, and his tail freed of bits of straw, cockleburs, and mud. The pennon on his lance needed a stitch or two, and his underwear lacked several buttons. And all these things, which in the past had scarcely held him up for so much as a day, now dragged themselves out for weeks.

But the time came when there was nothing left to do; and it was no longer possible for Sir Henry to delay his departure, without giving it up altogether. And with a curiously heavy heart, he went to say goodbye for the last time to Simpkins, and to his garden, and to the ducks in the moat.

"Goodbye," he said; "I am committed to my destiny, which is to be a hero; but I do not look forward to it. If anyone were to ask me, I would rather stay home."

And he went to find Alisane, who was busy cooking a gruel for Abigail. "Are you quite sure you want me to go?" he asked. "Now let me see," said Alisane, measuring: "one spoonful of salt, one cup of milk. . . ."

"I don't have to go," said Sir Henry. "If I could be of use here. . . ."

"My dear," said Alisane, "you must do as you like. You have always gone questing in the spring; why should you give it up, if it pleases you? We'll manage very well, Meghan and I. Don't worry about us."

"I wasn't really worrying," said Sir Henry. "I only meant . . ."

"With all the world riding," said Alisane, "it would be a pity to stay behind. The grand meetings . . . I know just how you feel."

"What I meant was . . ." said Sir Henry. . . .

"And after all," said Alisane, "summer is an easy time in a place like this, and we are well defended by the moat; and Meghan is very handy with the bow. But I have forgotten something." With this, she left him suddenly and went into her own room, and returned in a minute with a pair of warm woolen socks, which she held out to him. "Here," she said; "I knitted these for you, to wear in the woods at night." "Thank you, my dear," said Sir Henry. "That was very thoughtful of you." "They will keep you from catching a cold," said Alisane.

And she turned back to her gruel again. "One cup of milk," she said; "a teaspoonful of sweetening. . . .

"And then there is Manfred, too," she said. "He will guard us, while you are gone."

"I had expected to take Manfred with me," said Sir Henry. "I doubt if he would go," said Alisane.

"One cup of milk; a teaspoonful of sweetening. . . ."

"Well," said Sir Henry heavily, "if that's the way it is. . . ."

And approaching Alisane, he kissed her tenderly upon the brow, which was all she offered him. "Goodbye," he said, "dear wife. I will think of you very often, and send you news of me whenever I can." "Yes, do," said Alisane.

"This is my last quest," said Sir Henry. "I shall not go out again. Thank you for the socks."

Alisane put down her measuring spoon, and turned to him. "My dear," she said, "you have always wanted it both ways—both sweet and sour, like a pudding. I can see that you are going to feel sorry for yourself, whatever you do; but you will be better off moping in the woods by yourself than here at home. And I should rather have you homesick in some far-off corner of Lyonesse, than sick for Tintagel or Camelot, here among the ducks and the sheep."

She was silent for a moment, regarding him gravely. "I shall miss you, Henry," she said, "for I've grown used to having you about, and in many ways you've been a comfort to me. You have been a dear husband, even though never rightly wed; and if anything were to happen to you . . .

"Take care of yourself," she said, and went to him and kissed him quickly, and turned away.

[*177*]

"One teaspoonful of sweetening," she said, a little unsteadily; "and two of water. . . ."

But after a moment she put her measure down. "Don't just stand there," she cried; "go away!"

Sir Henry wiped a little drop of moisture from his eye, and went out to saddle Ponderer. Then he looked for Meghan, to say goodbye to her; but she was out, counting the new lambs among the sheep. "Manfred!" he called; "to heel!" But Manfred had seen how Ponderer was weighed down with all the furniture of a quest, the shield and helmet, the sword and the spear, the feather bed, the woolen underwear; and he had gone off to hide behind a tree.

So Sir Henry started out alone on his last journey. And because his heart was heavy, and he felt lonely, he tried to think of all the fine things waiting for him at Tintagel or Camelot, the great throng of knights, the stories and tales sung and embroidered, the feasting and the jousts, the rich stalls in the market places, the pride and the glory of his calling. And because he was going alone, he also tried to call to mind certain maidens he remembered having seen at one time or another; but Alisane's sweet face kept coming into his mind instead, and then Meghan's merry look, and then Alisane, and then Meghan again. And suddenly, to his astonishment, he found himself thinking of Abigail, his daughter; and he remembered her pretty ways with the porridge whenever she did not throw it on the floor; and with a groan, he exclaimed:

"What has gone wrong with me? I was never this way before."

Now that he was out, and away from home, a great homesickness came over him for his comfortable little castle with the moat and the tower he had built himself, and for Alisane, who had always been so good to him. "If only I were back," he thought, "watching her busy herself with her needle, and listening to Meghan's stories about distant lands and great deeds beyond the western sea."

But then he remembered that Meghan had not even been there to say goodbye to him, and that it had been a long while since Alisane had mended anything for him; and he felt suddenly frightened, and very lonely. And reining in his horse, he thought that he would turn about, and go back home again.

But he could not make up his mind; because he saw how absurd he would look, returning the very same day he had started; and he could imagine how Alisane would be vexed, and Meghan disappointed. And so he decided to stay out for one night, and to go home in the morning; but he did not expect to enjoy it.

Alas, poor Henry.

xviii

wherein he meets Himself

HE sat before his dying fire, listening to the night sounds in the forest around him. For once they did not comfort him. He sat with his chin on his hands, and his elbows on his knees, staring into the coals, and wondering at his own unease. "I am not ordinarily so anxious," he thought, "or, at least, not without good cause. I am not usually frightened of the dark, or of being alone; but to-night there is something in the forest. And I am not as young as I was, and my sword arm is rusty from lack of practice."

The night was spring-damp and misty, and after a while it seemed to Sir Henry that he could make out strange shapes in the mist. And as he stared at them, they seemed to come together into one Shape, dimly seen, but frightening and horrid. Sir Henry's knees knocked one upon the other, and he drew his shield up in front of him. "Who are you?" he cried into the darkness.

A voice rolled back at him:

"I am your enemy, Henry of Brentwood."

"You know my name," said Sir Henry; "but I do not know yours. Are you ogre, cockatrice, wizard, or knight?"

"I am what I am," said the voice. "And my name is known to you, Henry. It is Himself."

"I will not do battle with you," said Sir Henry.

"You cannot help it," said the Shape. "I will turn back sooner," said Sir Henry. "It will not save you," said the Shape, "for in whatever direction you go, you will find me going in the other. Turn back to Alisane, and you will find me with Meghan; or fly to Meghan, and I am with Alisane." "I often wish there were but one of them," said Sir Henry, "for

I am torn in two like Alyot. I will go on to Camelot."

"Then you must do battle with me," said the Shape, "for I bar your way in every direction."

"It seems to me that I have heard your voice somewhere before," said Sir Henry. "It is the sound of your own voice that you hear," said the Shape. "Yes," said Sir Henry; "and I do not like it." "I know," said Himself: "you have always preferred distant singing, and the sound of peace."

"So you remember that," said Sir Henry. "It was at Devizes."

"It was," agreed the Shape. "And you were quite eloquent. But you wounded Alisane to the heart, who loved you; and Meghan too." "Did they truly?" asked Sir Henry, wistfully. "I was reluctant to believe it; for I could not think so well of myself." "You never believed what was under your nose," said the Shape.

Sir Henry sighed. "Must I really fight you?" he asked. "I have a feeling that we could be friends."

"It is too late for that," said Himself, "so draw your sword."

Sir Henry held his sword in his hand, and his shield before him. But as the Shape advanced upon him he felt his heart turn to water in his breast. "I have little stomach for this," he said. "It is a gruesome encounter."

It seemed to Sir Henry that the night had grown even darker; and in the darkness the Shape appeared now here and now there, loomed huge and menacing above him, or disappeared without a sound into the shadows. And each time the Shape came at him, he brought with him the foul odor of fear; and each stroke of Sir Henry's sword cut through the air and the mist, and nothing else. But he himself counted the blows upon his armor, and those which cut through the old and rusty mail, to wound him near his heart. "Where are you?" he cried into the mist, trying to pierce the darkness between himself and his enemy; "Stand still; I cannot see you."

"You have never seen me, Henry," said the Shape. "Yet I have never been far from you, in your own perplexity of mind." "Am I to fight a giant in the dark?" cried Sir Henry. "You should never have let me grow so great," said Himself.

A moment later, Sir Henry felt his foe's sword sheer through the battered steel of his helmet, and bite deeply into the bone of his head. Weak with pain, and half blinded, he fell back a pace, and sank to one knee, behind his shield.

"Now I do regret that I was never wed to Alisane," he said, "for it would be a sweet thing to remember." "You might have been," said the Shape, "for there was a cathedral in Chichester, where you stopped." "It had a handsome window," said Sir Henry, "in three colors, and the altar was lit with many tapers. And there was a chapel, for small occasions. I wish I had the memory of it, in this hour." "It was too close at hand," said the Shape. "That was the trouble."

Sir Henry lay stretched out on the earth, with a

mortal wound in his heart. And it seemed to him that Alisane was there, bending over him. "I am dying," he whispered; "dear Alisane." "You were not lucky this time, my darling," she said. "No one is lucky against himself," said Sir Henry.

And then it was Meghan's face he saw above him, smiling at him gaily and tenderly. "Well now," she said, "you will see the Grail after all." "Why, so I will," said Sir Henry; "and I will think of Abigail's little silver porringer."

He was silent, drowning for a while in pain; and the perspiration ran down his face. "You must forgive me, ladies," he said at last, "if I make the rest of my journey without you. For where I am going no one goes save alone, and without weapons or armor of any kind. I am not afraid; for I am comforted that all things, both high and low, go upon that same journey . . . king, commoner, unicorn, and ant. And you also, my dear loves; and in her time, my daughter, who will remember only my name, and will not recognize me in the hereafter.

And there must surely be an hereafter, for if I did not meet with you again, I should wonder very much what I had done upon this earth. So there, you see; I am still thinking of yesterday and of to-morrow. So hold me in your hands for a little while, whilst I commend my spirit to God, who will expect it to be purified before it reaches Him; there was little evil in it, only foolishness."

He was silent and motionless for a long time. Before the hour of dawn, he made one more remark:

"It has a sound of peace," he said.

They found him the next day, lying under a tree. There were no wounds upon his body; and he was generally considered to have died of a seizure of the heart. He was buried in August in a vault in a small chapel which Meghan herself had built from stones from the tower. At Meghan's entreaty, his hot-water-bottle was buried with him; at Alisane's request, his one silver spur.

A NOTE ON THE TYPE IN WHICH
THIS BOOK IS SET

The text of this book is set in Caledonia, a Linotype face that belongs to the family of printing types called "modern face" by printers—a term used to mark the change in style of type-letters that occurred about 1800. Caledonia borders on the general design of Scotch Modern, but is more freely drawn than that letter.

The book was composed, printed, and bound by H. Wolff, New York. Typography and binding based on designs by W. A. Dwiggins.